Weaving the magic cloak

QUEEN ZIXI OF IX

OR THE STORY OF THE MAGIC CLOAK

by
L. Frank Baum

ILLUSTRATED BY
FREDERICK RICHARDSON

WITH A NEW INTRODUCTION BY
MARTIN GARDNER

DOVER PUBLICATIONS, INC.
NEW YORK

Published in Canada by General Publishing Company, Ltd., 30 Lesmill Road, Don Mills, Toronto, Ontario.
Published in the United Kingdom by Constable and Company, Ltd., 10 Orange Street, London WC 2.

This Dover edition, first published in 1971, is an unabridged republication of the work originally published by The Century Company, New York, in 1905. Pictures which appeared in color in the original are here reproduced in black and white. A new introduction has been written by Martin Gardner especially for the Dover edition.

International Standard Book Number: 0-486-22691-3
Library of Congress Catalog Card Number: 72-142287

Manufactured in the United States of America
Dover Publications, Inc.
180 Varick Street
New York, N. Y. 10014

Introduction

———•———

IN THE fall of 1905, when *Queen Zixi of Ix* was first published by the Century Company, New York, Lyman Frank Baum was well on his way to becoming this country's leading author of fantasy for children. He had published his first two Oz books, *The Wonderful Wizard of Oz* and *The Marvelous Land of Oz* (both available as Dover reprints), and a variety of other books including five non-Oz fantasies: *A New Wonderland* (also a Dover reprint, under its later title *The Magical Monarch of Mo*), *Dot and Tot of Merryland, The Master Key, The Life and Adventures of Santa Claus,* and *The Enchanted Island of Yew.* Baum had also written two books of short stories: *Mother Goose in Prose* and *American Fairy Tales.* All these books, and others of less importance, had been published within a seven-year period.

Queen Zixi of Ix was first serialized in the children's magazine, *St. Nicholas,* from November, 1904, through October, 1905, with illustrations by Frederick Richardson. A Chicago-born artist, Richardson had been with the *Chicago Daily News* for fifteen years before moving to New York City in 1903. The pictures he drew for *St. Nicholas* were used again in the book, except for one picture showing Zixi begging the fairy queen to grant her wish. (This missing illustration is restored here on page 230.) Richardson's advertising poster for the book is reproduced below. *Queen Zixi* was the only book of Baum's illustrated by Richardson, although he did provide the art for one of Baum's short stories, "A Kidnapped Santa Claus" (*The Delineator,* December, 1904).

St. Nicholas was owned by the Century Company. In a 1912 letter to Reilly & Britton, Baum's Chicago publishers, Baum speaks of having sold the serial rights of *Queen Zixi* for $1,500. This included the Century Company's right to publish it in book form. The 1905 first edition, of which two states have been distinguished, had a light green cloth cover with pictures on the front and back in red and dark green. It was first reprinted by the Century Company in 1906 and that same year a similar edition was issued in London by Hodder & Stoughton.

The book is dedicated to Frank Joslyn Baum, the oldest of Baum's four sons. Russell P. MacFall, in his biography of Baum, *To Please a Child* (Reilly & Lee, 1961), which he wrote with the aid of Frank, quotes Baum's inscription in the copy of *Queen Zixi* that he gave to his son: "You are the last of my boys to have one of my books dedicated to you, but it was your own wish, and in waiting for this story perhaps you have not been unwise. In some ways *Queen Zixi* is my best effort, and nearer to the 'old-fashioned' fairy tale than anything I have yet accomplished."

Queen Zixi is indeed the most classical in form of all Baum's book-length fairy tales, and in MacFall's opinion, Baum's best book next to *The Wonderful Wizard of Oz*. Edward Wagenknecht, in his 1929 booklet *Utopia Americana* (the first critical study of Baum's Oz books), as well as in later writings, has praised *Queen Zixi* as one of the best fairy tales ever written by anyone. It is in direct line with earlier fantasies in which palace life is combined with fairy lore and outrageous humor. One thinks of Andrew Lang's *Prince Prigio* (1889) and its sequel *Prince Ricardo* (1893), which Baum may have read and consciously imitated. (*Prince Prigio* was in turn a deliberate imitation of Thackeray's *The Rose and the Ring;* Lang even mentions that his mythical land of Pantouflia is near to Thackeray's kingdom of Paflagonia.) Some of the traditional fairy-tale elements that Baum adopts in *Queen Zixi* are noted by MacFall: the magic wishing device used foolishly, the moralizing against vanity, the cruel foster mother (Aunt Rivette), and the Cinderella child (Fluff).

The name of Baum's kingdom, Noland (no-land), reminds one of Samuel Butler's *Erewhon* (with two letters switched, "Erewhon" is "nowhere" backward) and the Neverland (in the play, Never-Never Land) of J. M. Barrie's *Peter and Wendy.* According to the official map of Oz and its environs, by artist Dick Martin and cartographer James Haff, Noland is just across the northeast corner of the Deadly Desert that surrounds the rectangular-shaped Oz. Noland is bounded on the southeast by Merryland, on the west by Ix. (After Oz and Mo, Ix was Baum's third attempt to catch the public's fancy with a two-letter word of his own invention; he was still reluctant to continue his Oz series.)

Ix and Noland are separated by high mountains, though not as high as the giant stair-step mountains in the northern part of Noland where the evil Roly-Rogues lived before they bounced down to capture Nole, the capital of Noland. The river into which these green, yellow, red, and brown soccerball monsters were finally rolled remains nameless, but the map by Haff and Martin shows that it carried them into the Nonestic Ocean which Dorothy was destined to cross in the third Oz book, *Ozma of Oz* (1907). They finally settled on Roly-Rogues Island, not far from Noland's northern coast.

The Forest of Burzee, which Baum had previously introduced in his *Life and Adventures of Santa Claus,* is across the Deadly Desert opposite the central southern boundary of Glinda's Quadling region of Oz. Glinda and Ozma later attend a conference there, with the fairies of Burzee, in Jack Snow's *The Magical Mimics in Oz.*

Queen Zixi, Bud, and Fluff are guests at Ozma's birthday party at the close of Baum's fifth Oz book, *The Road to Oz.* Dorothy guesses Zixi's age to be sixteen, but the Wizard whispers that she is actually thousands of years old. (The Wizard was either exaggerating or mistaken; we are told here on page 103 that Zixi's age is a mere 683.) In Baum's *The Magic of Oz,* Kiki Aru, in the form of a hawk, flies over Noland and Ix, with brief stopovers in each before he continues his westward flight to Ev. Noland and Ix are also mentioned in several post-Baum Oz books. Boxwood, an Ixian forest ruled by Chillywalla and inhabited by creatures made of boxes, is visited by the adventurers in Ruth Plumly Thompson's *The Silver Princess in Oz.* In her earlier book *The Wishing Horse of Oz,* Miss Thompson tells of Skampavia, a small country bordering on both Ix and Merryland. It is ruled by King Skamperoo, a power-hungry scamp who tries to conquer Oz after finding himself unwilling to invade nearby Ix because Zixi is much too friendly and pretty. Although the Roly-Rogues do not reappear in any later Oz book, their ability to roll and rebound was used again by Baum in his next non-Oz fantasy, *John Dough and the Cherub;* one of its creatures is Para Bruin, a rubber bear who likes to bunch himself into a ball and bounce from high places.

The word play in *Queen Zixi* is typical of Baum. The king's five fat counselors have names that differ only by the five vowels. On page 20 we are told that if the bell is tolled the people will be told of the king's death. Tollydob, the lord high general, becomes on page 91 a lord *very* high general when he grows ten feet tall. Zixi's assumed name, "Miss Trust," implies that she is to be mistrusted, as Baum makes clear on page 186. Bud's exclamation, "Fudge!" (page 210), is another amusing bit of word play. There is a touch of Carrollian logical nonsense on page 97. After Ruffles, a shaggy dog, has reminded Tallydab that talking dogs are common in fairy tales, he is told by Tallydab that "this isn't a fairy tale, Ruffles. It's real life in the kingdom of Noland." The old law of Noland that provides for giving the crown randomly to the forty-seventh person who enters the city's gate is splendid whimsy, but is it really any more random or whimsical than the ancient practice, once believed by millions to be divinely ordained, of passing the crown to a king's eldest son?

Richardson, who illustrated *Queen Zixi,* was a slightly built, gray-eyed man who studied art at the St. Louis School of Fine Arts in St. Louis, Missouri, and the Academie Julien in Paris. For seven years he taught at the Chicago Art Institute. He was strongly influenced by the Art Nouveau movement that flourished in the 1890's in England, Europe, and America, and which has had a recent revival in the United States in the current interest in Aubrey Beardsley, Tiffany glass, and the swirling, writhing patterns of psychedelic poster art. Selections from Richardson's elaborate pen-and-ink sketches for the *Chicago Daily News* were published in

Frederick Richardson's advertising poster
for "Queen Zixi of Ix."

Chicago by the Lakeside Press in 1899 with the title, *Book of Drawings.*

Queen Zixi was probably the first children's book Richardson illustrated. Later he did many others. The most elaborate was his *Mother Goose,* published by Volland in 1915 and still obtainable under an M. A. Donohue imprint. It contains more than a hundred full-color plates. Richardson also illustrated an *Aesop's Fables,* a *Pinocchio,* a volume of tales by Hans Christian Andersen, a little book of familiar short stories (such as The Three Bears) called *Old, Old Tales Retold,* a book of Indian folk tales, a book of Japanese folk tales, and many other books for children including a series of elementary school textbooks called *The Winston Readers.* He illustrated Frank Stockton's *The Queen's Museum and Other Fanciful Tales.* Richardson died in New York City on January 15, 1937, survived by Allan Barbour Richardson, one of his two sons, now retired and living in Winchester, Virginia.

Baum's single attempt at science fiction, *The Master Key,* weaves an adventure story around several marvelous scientific inventions which are given to a boy by the Demon of Electricity and misused by him. The story's moral, even more appropriate today, is that science is rapidly providing "gifts" too dangerous for humanity, in its present immature state, to handle wisely. I doubt if Baum had a similar moral in mind for the magic cloak in *Queen Zixi,* but it is amusing nonetheless to take the cloak as a symbol of science. The golden thread that gives the shimmering cloth its magic power is the method of induction. The fairies of Burzee offer the cloak to suffering mortals to make them happy; instead, it is used so foolishly that the immortals are obliged to withdraw it.

Pressing this metaphor, we can see General Tollydob's great height as the awesome power science has given today's generals. Aunt Rivette's wings are symbols of airplanes and spacecraft. Jikki's six ubiquitous, identical servants are the mass-produced robots of an automated age; they are even numbered like the names of modern computers. Tellydeb's long arm is, of course, the long reach of science, not only into the depths of space but also into the depths of the microworld. Tillydib's royal purse, always filled with gold, represents the fabulous riches of a scientific technology. Even the talking ability of Ruffles—to twist the metaphor still more—calls to mind the efforts of certain zoologists to converse with dolphins. Of course, the allegory breaks down at many points. The cloak's magic power, for example, fails to work if the cloak is stolen, whereas the secrets of science obviously work whether stolen or not.

The main moral of *Queen Zixi,* and one that Baum clearly intended, is that it is vain and foolish to desire the impossible. The moral is underlined by Zixi's conversations with the owl who wants to be a fish, the alligator who weeps crocodile tears because he cannot climb a tree, the ferryman's little girl who longs to be a man. Zixi is, of course, afflicted with the same foolishness. The golden-haired, black-eyed girl is not content to remain young and beautiful in her external appearance; she wants also to stay forever young and beautiful in a more fundamental sense that is belied by her haglike reflection in a mirror. She is the symbol of that ultimate of vanities, the desire of a mortal to escape earthly mortality.

In 1914 Baum's own motion picture firm, The Oz Film Manufacturing Company, made and released *The Magic Cloak of Oz,* a five-reeler based on *Queen Zixi.* Fluff was played by Mildred Harris, a twelve-year-old girl who four years later became Charlie Chaplin's first wife. The film—surprisingly good considering its time and how quickly it was made—closely follows Baum's text and Richardson's illustrations.

The book's first sentence, with "of Oz" added to "fairies," opens the screen play. Departures from the book include a beast called the Zoop, brief glimpses of the wooden Woozy (from *The Patchwork Girl of Oz,* which Baum had filmed earlier), and a band of robbers who steal Nikodemus, Aunt Rivette's donkey. (The evil robbers are first seen playing jacks, with a caption telling us that they had previously stolen "a nice little girl named Mary.") A variety of technical tricks liven the film, such as running it backward to show the defeated Roly-Rogues rolling back *up* their mountain instead of into a river.

I wish to thank James Haff, David Greene, Dick Martin, Fred Meyer, and Allan Barbour Richardson for generously offering information and advice in preparing this introduction.

MARTIN GARDNER

Hastings-on-Hudson, New York
September, 1970

TO MY SON
FRANK JOSLYN BAUM

Contents

————— •• —————

QUEEN ZIXI
OF IX

CHAPTER I.

THE WEAVING OF THE MAGIC CLOAK.

THE fairies assembled one moonlit night in a pretty clearing of the ancient forest of Burzee.

The clearing was in the form of a circle, and all around stood giant oak and fir trees, while in the center the grass grew green and soft as velvet. If any mortal had ever penetrated so far into the great forest, and could have looked upon the fairy circle by daylight, he might perhaps have seen a tiny path worn in the grass by the feet of the dancing elves. For here, during the full of the moon, the famous fairy band, ruled by good Queen Lulea, loved to dance and make merry while the silvery rays flooded the clearing and caused their gauzy wings to sparkle with every color of the rainbow.

On this especial night, however, they were not dancing. For the queen had seated herself upon a little green mound, and while her band clustered about her she began to address the fairies in a tone of discontent.

" I am tired of dancing, my dears," said she.

"Every evening since the moon grew big and round we have come here to frisk about and laugh and disport ourselves; and although those are good things to keep the heart light, one may grow weary even of merrymaking. So I ask you to suggest some new way to divert both me and yourselves during this night."

"That is a hard task," answered one pretty sprite, opening and folding her wings slowly—as a lady toys with her fan. "We have lived through so many ages that we long ago exhausted everything that might be considered a novelty, and of all our recreations nothing gives us such continued pleasure as dancing."

"But I do not care to dance to-night!" replied Lulea, with a little frown.

"We might create something, by virtue of our fairy powers," suggested one who reclined at the feet of the queen.

"Ah, that is just the idea!" exclaimed the dainty Lulea, with brightening countenance. "Let us create something. But what?"

"I have heard," remarked another member of the band, "of a thinking-cap having been made by some fairies in America. And whatever mortal wore this thinking-cap was able to conceive the most noble and beautiful thoughts."

"That was indeed a worthy creation," cried the little queen. "What became of the cap?"

"The man who received it was so afraid some one else would get it and be able to think the same exquisite thoughts as himself that he hid it safely away—so safely that he himself never could think afterward where he had placed it."

"How unfortunate! But we must not make another thinking-cap, lest it meet a like fate. Cannot you suggest something else?"

"I have heard," said another, "of certain fairies who created a pair of enchanted boots, which would always carry their mortal wearer away from danger —and never into it."

"What a great boon to those blundering mortals!" cried the queen. "And whatever became of the boots?"

"They came at last into the possession of a great general who did not know their powers. So he wore them into battle one day, and immediately ran away, followed by all his men, and the fight was won by the enemy."

"But did not the general escape danger?"

"Yes—at the expense of his reputation. So he retired to a farm and wore out the boots tramping up and down a country road and trying to decide why he had suddenly become such a coward."

"The boots were worn by the wrong man, surely," said the queen; "and that is why they proved a curse rather than a blessing. But we want no enchanted boots. Think of something else."

"Suppose we weave a magic cloak," proposed Espa, a sweet little fairy who had not before spoken.

"A cloak? Indeed, we might easily weave that," returned the queen. "But what sort of magic powers must it possess?"

"Let its wearer have any wish instantly fulfilled," said Espa, brightly.

"Suppose we weave a magic cloak."

But at this there arose quite a murmur of protest on all sides, which the queen immediately silenced with a wave of her royal hand.

"Our sister did not think of the probable consequences of what she suggested," declared Lulea, smiling into the downcast face of little Espa, who seemed to feel rebuked by the disapproval of the others. "An instant's reflection would enable her to see that such power would give the cloak's mortal wearer as many privileges as we ourselves possess. And I suppose you intended the magic cloak for a mortal wearer?" she inquired.

"Yes," answered Espa, shyly; "that was my intention."

"But the idea is good, nevertheless," continued the queen, "and I propose we devote this evening to weaving the magic cloak. Only, its magic shall give to its wearer the fulfilment of but one wish; and I am quite sure that even that should prove a great boon to the helpless mortals."

"Suppose more than one person wears the cloak," one of the band said; "which then shall have the one wish fulfilled?"

The queen devoted a moment to thought, and then replied:

"Each possessor of the magic cloak may have one wish granted, provided the cloak is not stolen from its last wearer. In that case the magic power will not be exercised on behalf of the thief."

"But should there not be a limit to the number of the cloak's wearers?" asked the fairy lying at the queen's feet.

"I think not. If used properly our gift will prove of great value to mortals. And if we find it is misused we can at any time take back the cloak and revoke its magic power. So now, if we are all agreed upon this novel amusement, let us set to work."

At these words the fairies sprang up eagerly; and their queen, smiling upon them, waved her wand toward the center of the clearing. At once a beautiful fairy loom appeared in the space. It was not such a loom as mortals use. It consisted of a large and a small ring of gold, supported by a tall pole of jasper. The entire band danced around it thrice, the fairies carrying in each hand a silver shuttle wound with glossy filaments finer than the finest silk. And the threads on each shuttle appeared a different hue from those of all the other shuttles.

At a sign from the queen they one and all approached the golden loom and fastened an end of thread in its warp. Next moment they were gleefully dancing hither and thither, while the silver shuttles flew swiftly from hand to hand and the gossamer-like web began to grow upon the loom.

Presently the queen herself took part in the sport, and the thread she wove into the fabric was the magical one which was destined to give the cloak its wondrous power.

Long and swiftly the fairy band worked beneath the old moon's rays, while their feet tripped gracefully over the grass and their joyous laughter tinkled like silver bells and awoke the echoes of the grim forest surrounding them. And at last they paused and threw themselves upon the green with little sighs of content.   For the shuttles and loom had vanished; the work was complete; and Queen Lulea stood upon the mound holding in her hand the magic cloak.

The garment was as beautiful as it was marvelous —each and every hue of the rainbow glinted and sparkled from the soft folds; and while it was light in weight as swan's-down, its strength was so great that the fabric was well-nigh indestructible.

The fairy band regarded it with great satisfaction, for every one had assisted in its manufacture and could admire with pardonable pride its glossy folds.

"It is very lovely, indeed!" cried little Espa. "But to whom shall we present it?"

The question aroused a dozen suggestions, each fairy seeming to favor a different mortal.   Every member of this band, as you doubtless know, was the unseen guardian of some man or woman or child in the great world beyond the forest, and it was but natural that each should wish her own ward to have the magic cloak.

While they thus disputed, another fairy joined them and pressed to the side of the queen.

"Welcome, Ereol," said Lulea.   "You are late."

The new-comer was very lovely in appearance, and with her fluffy golden hair and clear blue eyes was marvelously fair to look upon.   In a low, grave voice she answered the queen:

"Yes, your Majesty, I am late. But I could not help it. The old King of Noland, whose guardian I have been since his birth, has passed away this evening, and I could not bear to leave him until the end came."

"So the old king is dead at last!" said the queen, thoughtfully. "He was a good man, but woefully

"Yes, your Majesty, I am late."

uninteresting; and he must have wearied you greatly at times, my sweet Ereol."

"All mortals are, I think, wearisome," returned the fairy, with a sigh.

"And who is the new King of Noland?" asked Lulea.

"There is none," answered Ereol. "The old king

died without a single relative to succeed to his throne, and his five high counselors were in a great dilemma when I came away."

"Well, my dear, you may rest and enjoy yourself for a period, in order to regain your old lightsome spirits. By and by I will appoint you guardian to some newly born babe, that your duties may be less arduous. But I am sorry you were not with us to-night, for we have had rare sport. See! we have woven a magic cloak."

Ereol examined the garment with pleasure.

"And who is to wear it?" she asked.

Then again arose the good-natured dispute as to which mortal in all the world should possess the magic cloak. Finally the queen, laughing at the arguments of her band, said to them:

"Come! Let us leave the decision to the Man in the Moon. He has been watching us with a great deal of amusement, and once, I am sure, I caught him winking at us in quite a roguish way."

At this every head was turned toward the moon; and then a man's face, full-bearded and wrinkled, but with a jolly look upon the rough features, appeared sharply defined upon the moon's broad surface.

"So I 'm to decide another dispute, eh?" said he, in a clear voice. "Well, my dears, what is it this time?"

"We wish you to say what mortal shall wear the magic cloak which I and the ladies of my court have woven," replied Queen Lulea.

"Give it to the first unhappy person you meet," said the Man in the Moon. "The happy mortals have no need of magic cloaks." And with this advice the

"Give it to the first unhappy
person you meet,"
said the
Man in the Moon.

friendly face of the Man in the Moon faded away until only the outlines remained visible against the silver disk.

The queen clapped her hands delightedly.

"Our Man in the Moon is very wise," she declared;

"and we shall follow his suggestion. Go, Ereol, since you are free for a time, and carry the magic cloak to Noland. And the first person you meet who is really unhappy, be it man, woman, or child, shall receive from you the cloak as a gift from our fairy band."

Ereol bowed, and folded the cloak over her arm.

"Come, my children," continued Lulea; "the moon is hiding behind the tree-tops, and it is time for us to depart."

A moment later the fairies had disappeared, and the clearing wherein they had danced and woven the magic cloak lay shrouded in deepest gloom.

Chapter II.

THE BOOK OF LAWS.

On this same night great confusion and excitement prevailed among the five high counselors of the kingdom of Noland. The old king was dead and there was none to succeed him as ruler of the country. He had outlived every one of his relatives, and since the crown had been in this one family for generations, it puzzled the high counselors to decide upon a fitting successor.

These five high counselors were very important men. It was said that they ruled the kingdom while the king ruled them; which made it quite easy for the king and rather difficult for the people. The chief counselor was named Tullydub. He was old and very pompous, and had a great respect for the laws of the land. The next in rank was Tollydob, the lord high general of the king's army. The third was Tillydib, the lord high purse-bearer. The fourth was Tallydab, the lord high steward. And the fifth and last of the high counselors was Tellydeb, the lord high executioner.

These five had been careful not to tell the people when the old king had become ill, for they feared being annoyed by many foolish questions. They sat in a big room next the bed-chamber of the king, in the royal palace of Nole,—which is the capital city of Noland,—and kept every one out except the king's physician, who was half blind and wholly dumb and could not gossip with outsiders had he wanted to. And while the high counselors sat and waited for the king to recover or die, as he might choose, Jikki waited upon them and brought them their meals.

Jikki was the king's valet and principal servant. He was as old as any of the five high counselors; but they were all fat, whereas Jikki was wonderfully lean and thin; and the counselors were solemn and dignified, whereas Jikki was terribly nervous and very talkative.

"Beg pardon, my masters," he would say every five minutes, "but do you think his Majesty will get well?" And then, before any of the high counselors could collect themselves to answer, he continued: "Beg pardon, but do you think his Majesty will die?" And the next moment he would say: "Beg pardon, but do you think his Majesty is any better or any worse?"

And all this was so annoying to the high counselors that several times one of them took up some object in the room with the intention of hurling it at Jikki's head; but before he could throw it the old servant had nervously turned away and left the room.

Tellydeb, the lord high executioner, would often sigh: "I wish there were some law that would permit me to chop off Jikki's head." But then Tullydub, the chief counselor, would say gloomily: "There is no law but the king's will, and he insists that Jikki be allowed to live."

So they were forced to bear with Jikki as best they could; but after the king breathed his last breath the old servant became more nervous and annoying than ever.

Hearing that the king was dead, Jikki made a rush for the door of the bell-tower, but tripped over the foot of Tollydob and fell upon the marble floor so violently that his bones rattled, and he picked himself up half dazed by the fall.

"Where are you going?" asked Tollydob.

"To toll the bell for the king's death," answered Jikki.

"Well, remain here until

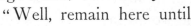

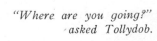

*"Where are you going?"
asked Tollydob.*

we give you permission to go," commanded the lord high general.

"But the bell ought to be tolled!" said Jikki.

"Be silent!" growled the lord high purse-bearer. "We know what ought to be done and what ought not to be done."

But this was not strictly true. In fact, the five high counselors did not know what ought to be done under these strange circumstances.

If they told the people the king was dead, and did not immediately appoint his successor, then the whole population would lose faith in them and fall to fighting and quarreling among themselves as to who should become king; and that would never in the world do.

No; it was evident that a new king must be chosen before they told the people that the old king was dead.

But whom should they choose for the new king? That was the important question.

While they talked of these matters, the ever-active Jikki kept rushing in and saying:

"Had n't I better toll the bell?"

"No!" they would shout in a chorus; and then Jikki would rush out again.

So they sat and thought and counseled together during the whole long night, and by morning they were no nearer a solution of the problem than before.

At daybreak Jikki stuck his head into the room

and said:

"Had n't I better—"

"No!" they all shouted in a breath.

"Very well," returned Jikki; "I was only going to ask if I had n't better get you some breakfast."

"Yes!" they cried, again in one breath.

"And shall I toll the bell?"

"No!" they screamed; and the lord high steward threw an inkstand that hit the door several seconds after Jikki had closed it and disappeared.

While they were at breakfast they again discussed their future action in the choice of a king; and finally the chief counselor had a thought that caused him to start so suddenly that he nearly choked.

"The book!" he gasped, staring at his brother counselors in a rather wild manner.

"What book?" asked the lord high general.

"The book of laws," answered the chief counselor.

"I never knew there was such a thing," remarked the lord high executioner, looking puzzled. "I always thought the king's will was the law."

"So it was! So it was when we had a king," answered Tullydub, excitedly. "But this book of laws was written years ago, and was meant to be used when the king was absent, or ill, or asleep."

For a moment there was silence.

"Have you ever read the book?" then asked Tillydib.

"No; but I will fetch it at once, and we shall see

Suddenly placing his broad thumb on a passage, he shouted: "I have it! I have it!"

if there is not a law to help us out of our difficulty."

So the chief counselor brought the book—a huge

old volume that had a musty smell to it and was locked together with a silver padlock. Then the key had to be found, which was no easy task; but finally the great book of laws lay open upon the table, and all the five periwigs of the five fat counselors were bent over it at once.

Long and earnestly they searched the pages, but it was not until after noon that Tullydub suddenly placed his broad thumb upon a passage and shouted:

"I have it! I have it!"

"What is it? Read it! Read it aloud!" cried the others.

So the counselor brought the book.

Just then Jikki rushed into the room and asked: "Shall I toll the bell?"

"No!" they yelled, glaring at him; so Jikki ran out, shaking his head dolefully.

Then Tullydub adjusted his spectacles and leaned over the book, reading aloud the following words:

"In case the king dies, and there is no one to succeed him, the chief counselor of the kingdom shall go at sunrise to the eastward gate of the city of Nole

"No!" they all shouted in a breath.

and count the persons who enter through such gate as soon as it is opened by the guards. And the forty-seventh person that so enters, be it man, woman, or child, rich or poor, humble or noble, shall immediately be proclaimed king or queen, as the case may be, and shall rule all the kingdom of Noland forever after, so long as he or she may live. And if any one in all the kingdom of Nole shall refuse to obey the slightest wish of the new ruler, such person shall at once be put to death. This is the law."

Then all the five high counselors heaved a deep

sigh of relief and repeated together the words:

"This is the law."

"But it 's a strange law, nevertheless," remarked the lord high purse-bearer. "I wish I knew who will be the forty-seventh person to enter the east gate to-morrow at sunrise."

"We must wait and see," answered the lord high general. "And I will have my army assembled and marshaled at the gateway, that the new ruler of Noland may be welcomed in a truly kingly manner, as well as to keep the people in order when they hear the strange news."

"Beg pardon!" exclaimed Jikki, looking in at the doorway, "but shall I toll the bell?"

"No, you numskull!" retorted Tullydub, angrily. "If the bell is tolled the people will be told, and they must not know that the old king is dead until the forty-seventh person enters the east gateway to-morrow morning!"

Chapter III.

THE GIFT OF THE MAGIC CLOAK.

NEARLY two days' journey from the city of Nole, yet still within the borders of the great kingdom of Noland, was a little village lying at the edge of a broad river. It consisted of a cluster of houses of the humblest description, for the people of this village were all poor and lived in simple fashion. Yet one house appeared to be somewhat better than the others, for it stood on the river-bank and had been built by the ferryman whose business it was to carry all travelers across the river. And, as many traveled that way, the ferryman was able in time to erect a very comfortable cottage, and to buy good furniture for it, and to clothe warmly and neatly his two children.

One of these children was a little girl named Margaret, who was called "Meg" by the villagers and "Fluff" by the ferryman her father, because her hair was so soft and fluffy.

Her brother, who was two years younger, was named Timothy; but Margaret had always called him "Bud," because she could not say "brother" more plainly when first she began to talk; so nearly every one who knew Timothy called him Bud, as little Meg did.

These children had lost their mother when very young, and the big ferryman had tried to be both mother and father to them, and had reared thcm very gently and lovingly. They were good children, and were liked by every one in the village.

But one day a terrible misfortune befell them. The ferryman tried to cross the river for a passenger one very stormy night; but he never reached the other shore. When the storm subsided and morning came they found his body lying on the river-bank, and the two children were left alone in the world.

The news was carried by travelers to the city of Nole, where the ferryman's only sister lived; and a few days afterward the woman came to the village and took charge of her orphaned niece and nephew.

She was not a bad-hearted woman, this Aunt Rivette; but she had worked hard all her life, and had a stern face and a stern voice. She thought the only way to make children behave was to box their ears every now and then; so poor Meg, who had been well-nigh heart-broken at her dear father's loss, had still more occasion for tears after Aunt Rivette came to the village.

As for Bud, he was so impudent and ill-mannered to the old lady that she felt obliged to switch him; and afterward the boy became surly and silent, and neither wept nor answered his aunt a single word. It hurt Margaret dreadfully to see her little brother whipped, and she soon became so unhappy at the sorrowful circumstances in which she and her brother found themselves that she sobbed from morning till night and knew no comfort.

Aunt Rivette, who was a laundress in the city of Nole, decided she would take Meg and Bud back home with her.

"The boy can carry water for my tubs, and the girl can help me with the ironing," she said.

So she sold all the heavier articles of furniture that the cottage contained, as well as the cottage itself; and all the remainder of her dead brother's belongings she loaded upon the back of the little donkey she had ridden on her journey from Nole. It made such a pile of packages that the load seemed bigger than the donkey himself; but he was a strong little animal, and made no complaint of his burden.

All this being accomplished, they set out one morning for Nole, Aunt Rivette leading the donkey by the bridle with one hand and little Bud with the other, while Margaret followed behind, weeping anew at this sad parting with her old home and all she had so long loved.

It was a hard journey. The old woman soon became cross and fretful, and scolded the little ones at almost every step. When Bud stumbled, as he often did, for he was unused to walking very far, Aunt Rivette would box his ears or shake him violently by the arm or tell him he was "a good-for-nothing little beggar." And Bud would turn upon her with a revengeful look in his big eyes, but say not a word. The woman paid no attention to Meg, who continued to follow the donkey with tearful eyes and drooping head.

The first night they obtained shelter at a farmhouse. But in the morning it was found that the boy's feet were so swollen and sore from the long

It was a hard journey.

walk of the day before that he could not stand upon them. So Aunt Rivette, scolding fretfully at his weakness, perched Bud among the bundles atop the donkey's back, and in this way they journeyed the

second day, the woman walking ahead and leading
the donkey, and Margaret following behind.

The laundress had hoped to reach the city of Nole
at the close of this day; but the overburdened donkey
would not walk very fast, so nightfall found them
still a two-hours' journey from the city gates, and
they were forced to stop at a small inn.

But this inn was already overflowing with travelers, and the landlord could give them no beds, nor
even a room.

"You can sleep in the stable if you like," said he.
"There is plenty of hay to lie down upon."

So they were obliged to content themselves with
this poor accommodation.

The old woman aroused them at the first streaks
of daybreak the next morning, and while she fastened
the packages to the donkey's back Margaret stood in
the stable yard and shivered in the cold morning air.

The little girl felt that she had never been more
unhappy than at that moment, and when she thought
of her kind father and the happy home she had once
known, her sobs broke out afresh, and she leaned
against the stable door and wept as if her little heart
would break.

Suddenly some one touched her arm, and she looked
up to see a tall and handsome youth standing before
her. It was none other than Ereol the fairy, who
had assumed this form for her appearance among
mortals; and over the youth's arm lay folded the

magic cloak that had been woven the evening before in the fairy circle of Burzee.

"Are you very unhappy, my dear?" asked Ereol, in kindly tones.

"I am the most unhappy person in all the world!" replied the girl, beginning to sob afresh.

"Then," said Ereol, "I will present you with this magic cloak, which has been woven by the fairies. And while you wear it you may have your first wish granted; and if you give it freely to any other mortal, that person may also have one wish granted. So use the cloak wisely, and guard it as a great treasure."

Saying this the fairy messenger spread the folds of the cloak and threw the brilliant-hued garment over the shoulders of the girl.

Just then Aunt Rivette led the donkey from the stable, and seeing the beautiful cloak which the child wore, she stopped short and demanded:

"Where did you get that?"

"This stranger gave it to me," answered Meg, pointing to the youth.

"Take it off! Take it off this minute and give it me—or I will whip you soundly!" cried the woman.

"Stop!" said Ereol, sternly. "The cloak belongs to this child alone, and if you dare take it from her I will punish you severely."

"What! Punish me! Punish me, you rascally fellow! We'll see about that."

"We will, indeed," returned Ereol, more calmly.

Over the youth's arm lay folded the magic cloak.

"The cloak is a gift from the fairies; and you dare not anger them, for your punishment would be swift and terrible."

Now no one feared to provoke the mysterious

F RICHARDSON

"What! Punish me, you rascally fellow! We'll see about that."

fairies more than Aunt Rivette; but she suspected the youth was not telling her the truth, so she rushed upon Ereol and struck at him with her upraised cane. But, to her amazement, the form of the youth vanished quickly into air, and then, indeed, she knew it was a fairy that had spoken to her.

"You may keep your cloak," she said to Margaret, with a little shiver of fear. "I would not touch it for the world!"

The girl was very proud of her glittering garment, and when Bud was perched upon the donkey's back and the old woman began trudging along the road to the city, Meg followed after with much lighter steps than before.

Presently the sun rose over the horizon, and its splendid rays shone upon the cloak and made it glisten gorgeously.

"Ah, me!" sighed the little girl, half aloud. "I wish I could be happy again!"

Then her childish heart gave a bound of delight, and she laughed aloud and brushed from her eyes the last tear she was destined to shed for many a day. For, though she spoke thoughtlessly, the magic cloak quickly granted to its first wearer the fulfilment of her wish.

Aunt Rivette turned upon her in surprise.

"What 's the matter with you?" she asked suspiciously, for she had not heard the girl laugh since her father's death.

"Why, the sun is shining," answered Meg, laughing again. "And the air is sweet and fresh, and the trees are green and beautiful, and the whole world is very pleasant and delightful." And then she danced lightly along the dusty road and broke into a verse of a pretty song she had learned at her father's knee.

The old woman scowled and trudged on again; Bud looked down at his merry sister and grinned

"Ah, me!" sighed the little girl, half aloud.

from pure sympathy with her high spirits; and the donkey stopped and turned his head to look solemnly at the laughing girl behind him.

"Come along!" cried the laundress, jerking at the bridle; "every one is passing us upon the road, and we must hurry to get home before noon."

It was true. A good many travelers, some on horseback and some on foot, had passed them by since the sun rose; and although the east gate of the city of Nole was now in sight, they were obliged to take their places in the long line that sought entrance at the gate.

CHAPTER IV.

KING BUD OF NOLAND.

THE five high counselors of the kingdom of Noland were both eager and anxious upon this important morning. Long before sunrise Tollydob, the lord high general, had assembled his army at the east gate of the city; and the soldiers stood in two long lines beside the entrance, looking very impressive in their uniforms. And all the people, noting this unusual display, gathered around at the gate to see what was going to happen.

Of course no one knew what was going to happen; not even the chief counselor nor his brother counselors. They could only obey the law and abide by the results.

Finally the sun arose and the east gate of the city was thrown open. There were a few people waiting outside, and they promptly entered.

"One, two, three, four, five, six!" counted the chief counselor, in a loud voice.

The people were much surprised at hearing this, and began to question one another with perplexed looks. Even the soldiers were mystified.

"Seven, eight, nine!" continued the chief counselor, still counting those who came in.

A breathless hush fell upon the assemblage.

Something very important and mysterious was going on; that was evident.   But what?

They could only wait and find out.

"Ten, eleven!" counted Tullydub, and then heaved

A ragged, limping peddler entered the gate.

a deep sigh.   For a famous nobleman had just entered the gate, and the chief counselor could not help wishing he had been number forty-seven.

So the counting went on, and the people became more and more interested and excited.

When the number had reached thirty-one a strange thing happened.   A loud "boom!" sounded through the stillness, and then another, and another. Some one was tolling the great bell in the palace bell-tower, and people began saying to one another in awed whispers that the old king must be dead.

The five high counselors, filled with furious anger but absolutely helpless, as they could not leave the gate, lifted up their five chubby fists and shook them violently in the direction of the bell-tower.

Poor Jikki, finding himself left alone in the palace, could no longer resist the temptation to toll the bell; and it continued to peal out its dull, solemn tones while the chief counselor stood by the gate and shouted:

"Thirty-two, thirty-three, thirty-four!"

Only the mystery of this action could have kept the people quiet when they learned from the bell that their old king was dead.

But now they began to guess that the scene at the east gate promised more of interest than anything they might learn at the palace; so they stood very quiet, and Jikki's disobedience of orders did no great harm to the plans of the five high counselors.

When Tullydub had counted up to forty the excitement redoubled, for every one could see big drops of perspiration standing upon the chief counselor's brow, and all the other high counselors, who stood just behind him, were trembling violently with nervousness.

A ragged, limping peddler entered the gate.

"Forty-five!" shouted Tullydub.

"Forty-seven!" cried the chief counselor. "Long live the new King of Noland!"

Then came Aunt Rivette, dragging at the bridle of the donkey.

"Forty-six!" screamed Tullydub.

And now Bud rode through the gate, perched among the bundles on the donkey's back and looking composedly upon the throng of anxious faces that greeted him.

"*Forty-seven!*" cried the chief counselor; and then in his loudest voice he continued:

"Long live the new King of Noland!"

All the high counselors prostrated themselves in the dusty road before the donkey. The old woman was thrust back in the crowd by a soldier, where she stood staring in amazement, and Margaret, clothed in her beautiful cloak, stepped to the donkey's side and looked first at her brother and then at the group of periwigged men, who bobbed their heads in the dust before him and shouted:

"Long live the king!"

Then, while the crowd still wondered, the lord high counselor arose and took from a soldier a golden crown set with brilliants, a jeweled scepter, and a robe of ermine. Advancing to Bud, he placed the crown upon the boy's head and the scepter in his hand, while over his shoulders he threw the ermine robe.

The crown fell over Bud's ears, but he pushed it back upon his head, so it would stay there; and as the kingly robe spread over all the bundles on the donkey's back and quite covered them, the boy really presented a very imposing appearance.

The people quickly rose to the spirit of the occasion. What mattered it if the old king was dead, now that a new king was already before them? They broke into a sudden cheer, and, joyously waving their hats and bonnets above their heads, joined eagerly in the cry:

"Long live the King of Noland!"

*"May it please your
Serene Majesty to tell us
who this young lady is?"
asked Tullydub, respectfully.*

Aunt Rivette was fairly stupefied. Such a thing was too wonderful to be believed. A man in the crowd snatched the bonnet from the old woman's head, and said to her brusquely:

"Why don't you greet the new king? Are you a traitor to your country?"

So she also waved her bonnet and screamed: "Long live the king!" But she hardly knew what she was doing or why she did it.

Meantime the high counselors had risen from their knees and now stood around the donkey.

" May it please your Serene Majesty to condescend to tell us who this young lady is?" asked Tullydub, bowing respectfully.

"That's my sister Fluff," said Bud, who was enjoying his new position very much.   All the counselors, at this, bowed low to Margaret.

"A horse for the Princess Fluff!" cried the lord high general; and the next moment she was mounted upon a handsome white palfrey, where, with her fluffy golden hair and smiling face and the magnificent cloak   flowing from her shoulders, she looked every inch a princess.   The people cheered her, too; for it was long since any girl or woman had occupied the

She screamed: "Long live the king!"

palace of the King of Noland, and she was so pretty and sweet that every one loved her immediately.

And now the king's chariot drove up, with its six prancing steeds, and Bud was lifted from the back of the donkey and placed in the high seat of the chariot.

Again the people shouted joyful greetings; the band struck up a gay march tune, and then the royal procession started for the palace.

First came Tollydob and his officers; then the king's chariot, surrounded by soldiers; then the four high counselors upon black horses, riding two on each side of Princess Fluff; and, finally, the band of musicians and the remainder of the royal army.

It was an imposing sight, and the people followed after with cheers and rejoicings, while the lord high purse-bearer tossed silver coins from his pouch for any one to catch who could.

A message had been sent to warn Jikki that the new king was coming, so he stopped tolling the death knell, and instead rang out a glorious chime of welcome.

As for old Rivette, finding herself and the donkey alike deserted, she once more seized the bridle and led the patient beast to her humble dwelling; and it was just as she reached her door that King Bud of Noland, amid the cheers and shouts of thousands, entered for the first time the royal palace of Nole.

CHAPTER V.

PRINCESS FLUFF.

Now when the new king had entered the palace
with his sister, the chief counselor stood upon a golden
balcony with the great book in his hand, and read
aloud, to all the people who were gathered below, the
law in regard to choosing a new king, and the severe
penalty in case any refused to obey his slightest wish.
And the people were glad enough to have a change
of rulers, and pleased that so young a king had been
given them.   So they accepted both the law and the
new king cheerfully, and soon dispersed to their homes
to talk over the wonderful events of the day.

Bud and Meg were ushered into beautifully fur-
nished rooms on the second floor of the palace, and
old Jikki, finding that he had a new master to serve,
flew about in his usual nervous manner, and brought
the children the most delicious breakfast they had
ever eaten in their lives.

Bud had been so surprised at his reception at the
gate and the sudden change in his condition that as
yet he had not been able to collect his thoughts. His
principal idea was that he was in a dream, and he

kept waiting until he should wake up. But the breakfast was very real and entirely satisfying, and he began to wonder if he could be dreaming, after all.

The old servant, when he carried away the dishes, bowed low to Bud and said: " Beg pardon, your Majesty! But the lord high counselor desires to know the king's will."

Bud stared at him a moment thoughtfully.

"Tell him I want to be left alone to talk with my sister Fluff," he replied.

Jikki again bowed low and withdrew, closing the door behind him, and then the children looked at each other solemnly, until Meg burst into a merry laugh.

"Oh, Bud!" she cried, "think of it! I 'm the royal Princess Fluff, and you 're the King of all Noland! Is n't it funny!" And then she danced about the room in great delight.

Bud answered her seriously.

"What does it all mean, Fluff?" he said. "We 're only poor children, you know; so I can't really be a king. And I would n't be surprised if Aunt Rivette came in any minute and boxed my ears."

"Nonsense!" laughed Margaret. "Did n't you hear what that fat, periwigged man said about the law? The old king is dead, and some one else had to be king, you know; and the forty-seventh person who entered the east gate was you, Bud, and so by

law you are the king of all this great country. Don't
you see?"

Bud shook his head and looked at his sister.

"No, I don't see," he said. "But if you say it's
all right, Fluff, why, it must be all right."

"Of course it's all right," declared the girl, throwing off her pretty cloak and placing it on a chair.
"You're the rightful king, and can do whatever you
please; and I'm the rightful princess, because I'm
your sister; so I can do whatever *I* please. Don't
you see, Bud?"

"But, look here, Fluff," returned her brother, "if
you're a princess, why do you wear that old gray
dress and those patched-up shoes? Father used to
tell us that princesses always wore the loveliest
dresses."

Meg looked at herself and sighed.

"I really ought to have some new dresses, Bud.
And I suppose if you order them they will be ready
in no time. And you must have some new clothes,
too, for your jacket is ragged and soiled."

"Do you really think it's true, Fluff?" he asked
anxiously.

"Of course it's true. Look at your kingly robe,
and your golden crown, and that stick with all those
jewels in it!"—meaning the scepter. "They're true
enough, are n't they?"

Bud nodded.

"Call in that old man," he said. "I'll order something, and see if he obeys me. If he does, then I 'll believe I 'm really a king."

"But now listen, Bud," said Meg, gravely; "don't you let these folks see you 're afraid, or that you 're not sure whether you 're a king or not. Order them around and make them afraid of *you.* That 's what the kings do in all the stories I ever read."

"I will," replied Bud. "I 'll order them around. So you call in that old donkey with the silver buttons all over him."

"Here 's a bell-rope," said Meg; "I 'll pull it."

Instantly Jikki entered and bowed low to each of the children.

"What 's your name?" asked Bud.

"Jikki, your gracious Majesty."

"Who are you?"

"Your Majesty's valet, if you please," answered Jikki.

"Oh!" said Bud. He did n't know what a valet was, but he was n't going to tell Jikki so.

"I want some new clothes, and so does my sister," Bud announced, as boldly as possible.

"Certainly, your Majesty. I 'll send the lord high steward here at once."

With this he bowed and rushed away, and presently Tallydab, the lord high steward, entered the room and with a low bow presented himself respectfully before the children.

"I beg your Majesty to command me," said Tallydab, gravely.

Bud was a little awed by his appearance, but he resolved to be brave.

"We want some new clothes," he said.

"They are already ordered, your Majesty, and will be here presently."

"I want some new clothes, and so does my sister," Bud announced, as boldly as possible.

"Oh!" said Bud, and stopped short.

"I have ordered twenty suits for your Majesty and forty gowns for the princess," continued Tallydab; "and I hope these will content your Majesty and the princess until you have time to select a larger assortment."

"Oh!" said Bud, greatly amazed.

"I have also selected seven maidens, the most

noble in all the land, to wait upon the princess.
They are even now awaiting her Highness in her
own apartments."

Meg clapped her hands delightedly.

*"I have ordered twenty suits for your Majesty and forty
gowns for the princess."*

"I 'll go to them at once," she cried.

"Has your Majesty any further commands?" asked
Tallydab. "If not your five high counselors would
like to confer with you in regard to your new duties
and responsibilities."

"Send 'em in," said Bud, promptly; and while Margaret went to meet her new maids the king held his first conference with his high counselors.

In answer to Tallydab's summons the other four periwigs, pompous and solemn, filed into the room and stood in a row before Bud, who looked upon them with a sensation of awe.

"Your Majesty," began the venerable Tullydub, in a grave voice, "we are here to instruct you, with your gracious consent, in your new and important duties."

Bud shifted uneasily in his chair. It all seemed so unreal and absurd—this kingly title and polite deference bestowed upon a poor boy by five dignified and periwigged men—that it was hard for Bud to curb his suspicion that all was not right.

"See here, all of you," said he, suddenly, "is this thing a joke? tell me, is it a joke?"

"A joke?" echoed all of the five counselors, in several degrees of shocked and horrified tones; and Tellydeb, the lord high executioner, added reproachfully:

"Could we, by any chance, have the temerity to joke with your mighty and glorious Majesty?"

"That's just it," answered the boy. "I am not a mighty and glorious Majesty. I 'm just Bud, the ferryman's son, and you know it."

"You are Bud, the ferryman's son, to be sure," agreed the chief counselor, bowing courteously; "but by the decrees of fate and the just and unalterable laws of the land you are now become absolute ruler of the great kingdom of Noland; therefore all that dwell therein are your loyal and obedient servants."

Bud thought this over.

"Are you sure there's no mistake?" he asked, with hesitation.

"A joke?" echoed all of the five counselors.

"There *can* be no mistake," returned old Tullydub, firmly; "for we, the five high counselors of the kingdom, have ourselves interpreted and carried out the laws of the land, and the people, your subjects, have approved our action."

"Then," said Bud, "I suppose I'll have to be king whether I want to or not."

"Your Majesty speaks but the truth," returned the chief counselor, with a sigh. "With or without your

consent, you are the king.   It is the law." And all
the others chanted in a chorus:

"It is the law."

Bud felt much relieved.   He had no notion whatever of refusing to be a king.   If there was no mistake, and he was really the powerful monarch of
Noland, then there ought to be no end of fun and
freedom for him during the rest of his life.   To be
his own master; to have plenty of money; to live in
a palace and order people around as he pleased—all
this seemed to the poor and friendless boy of yesterday to be quite the most delightful fate that could
possibly overtake one.

So lost did he become in thoughts of the marvelous existence opening before him that he paid scant
attention to the droning speeches of the five aged
counselors, who were endeavoring to acquaint him
with the condition of affairs in his new kingdom, and
to instruct him in his many and difficult duties as its
future ruler.

For a full hour he sat quiet and motionless, and
they thought he was listening to these dreary affairs
of state; but suddenly he jumped up and astonished
the dignitaries by exclaiming:

"See here; you just fix up things to suit yourselves.   I'm going to find Fluff." And with no
heed to protests, the new king ran from the room
and slammed the door behind him.

Chapter VI.

BUD DISPENSES JUSTICE.

THE next day the funeral of the old king took place, and the new king rode in the grand procession in a fine chariot, clothed in black velvet embroidered with silver. Not knowing how to act in his new position, Bud sat still and did nothing at all, which was just what was expected of him.

But when they returned from the funeral he was ushered into the great throne-room of the palace and seated on the golden throne; and then the chief counselor informed him that he must listen to the grievances of his people and receive the homage of the noblemen of Noland.

Fluff sat on a stool beside the king, and the five high counselors stood back of him in a circle; and then the doors were thrown open and all the noblemen of the country crowded in. One by one they kissed first the king's hand and then the princess's hand, and vowed they would always serve them faithfully.

Bud did not like this ceremony. He whispered to Fluff that it made him tired.

"I want to go upstairs and play," he said to the

lord high steward. " I don't see why I can't."

" Very soon your Majesty may go. Just now it is your duty to hear the grievances of your people," answered Tallydab, gently.

" What 's the matter with 'em ? " asked Bud, crossly. " Why don't they keep out of trouble ? "

" I do not know, your Majesty; but there are always disputes among the people."

" But that is n't the king's fault, is it ? " said Bud.

" No, your Majesty; but it 's the king's place to settle these disputes, for he has the supreme power."

" Well, tell 'em to hurry up and get it over with," said the boy, restlessly.

Then a venerable old man came in leading a boy by the arm and holding a switch in his other hand.

" Your Majesty," began the man, having first humbly bowed to the floor before the king, " my son, whom I have brought here with me, insists upon running away from home, and I wish you would tell me what to do with him."

" Why do you run away ? " Bud asked the boy.

" Because he whips me," was the answer.

Bud turned to the man.

" Why do you whip the boy ? " he inquired.

" Because he runs away," said the man.

For a minute Bud looked puzzled.

" Well, if any one whipped me, I 'd run away, too," he said at last. " And if the boy is n't whipped or abused he ought to stay at home and be good. But it 's none of my business, anyhow."

"Oh, your Majesty!" cried the chief counselor, "it really must be your business. You 're the king, you know; and everybody's business is the king's."

A man came in leading a boy by the arm and holding a switch in his other hand.

"That is n't fair," said Bud, sulkily. "I 've got my own business to attend to, and I want to go upstairs and play."

But now Princess Fluff leaned toward the young

king and whispered something in his ear which made his face brighten.

"See here!" exclaimed Bud, "the first time this man whips the boy again, or the first time the boy runs away, I order my lord high executioner to give

Next came two old women, and between them they led a cow.

them both a good switching. Now let them go home and try to behave themselves."

Every one applauded his decision, and Bud also thought with satisfaction that he had hit upon a good way out of the difficulty.

Next came two old women, one very fat and the other very thin; and between them they led a cow, the fat woman having a rope around one horn and the thin woman a rope around the other horn. Each woman claimed she owned the cow, and they quarreled so loudly and so long that the lord high executioner had to tie a bandage over their mouths. When peace was thus restored the high counselor said:

"Now, your Majesty, please decide which of these two women owns the cow."

"I can't," said Bud, helplessly.

"Oh, your Majesty, but you must!" cried all the five high counselors.

Then Meg whispered to the king again, and the boy nodded. The children had always lived in a little village where there were plenty of cows, and the girl thought she knew a way to decide which of the claimants owned this animal.

"Send one of the women away," said Bud. So they led the lean woman to a little room near by and locked her in.

"Bring a pail and a milking-stool," ordered the king.

When they were brought, Bud turned to the fat woman and ordered the bandage taken from her mouth.

"The cow's mine! It's my cow! I own it!" she screamed, the moment she could speak.

"Hold!" said the king. "If the cow belongs to you, let me see you milk her."

"Certainly, your Majesty, certainly!" she cried; and seizing the pail and the stool, she ran up to the left side of the cow, placed the stool, and sat down upon it. But before she could touch the cow the animal suddenly gave a wild kick that sent the startled woman in a heap upon the floor, with her head stuck fast in the milk-pail. Then the cow moved forward a few steps and looked blandly around.

Two of the guards picked the woman up and pulled

F. RICHARDSON

The animal suddenly gave a wild kick that sent the startled woman in a heap upon the floor, with her head stuck fast in the milk-pail.

the pail from her head.

"What 's the matter?" asked Bud.

"She 's frightened, of course," whimpered the woman, "and I 'll be black and blue by to-morrow morning, your Majesty. Any cow would kick in such a place as this."

"Put this woman in the room and fetch the other

woman here," commanded the king.

So the lean woman was brought out and ordered to milk the cow.

She took the stool in one hand and the pail in the other, and, approaching the cow softly on the *right* side, patted the animal gently and said to it: "So, Boss! So-o-o-o, Bossie, my darlin'! Good Bossie! Nice Bossie!"

The cow turned her head to look at the lean woman, and made no objection when she sat down and began milking.

In a moment the king said:

"The cow is yours! Take her and go home!"

Then all the courtiers and people—and even the five high counselors—applauded the king enthusiastically; and the chief counselor lifted up his hands and said:

"Another Solomon has come to rule us!"

And the people applauded again, till Bud looked very proud and quite red in the face with satisfaction.

"Tell me," he said to the woman, who was about to lead the cow away, "tell me, where did you get such a nice faithful Bossie as that?"

"Must I tell you the truth?" asked the woman.

"Of course," said Bud.

"Then, your Majesty," she returned, "I stole her from that fat woman you have locked up in that room. But no one can take the cow from me now, for the king has given her to me."

At this a sudden hush fell on the room, and Bud looked redder than ever.

"Then how did it happen that you could milk the cow and she could n't?" demanded the king, angrily.

"Why, she does n't understand cows, and I do," answered the woman. "Good day, your Majesty. Much obliged, I 'm sure!"

And she walked away with the cow, leaving the king and Princess Fluff and all the people much embarrassed.

"Have we any cows in the royal stables?" asked Bud, turning to Tullydub.

"Certainly, your Majesty; there are several," answered the chief counselor.

"Then," said Bud, "give one of them to the fat woman and send her home. I 've done all the judging I am going to do to-day, and now I 'll take my sister upstairs to play."

"Hold on! Hold on!" cried a shrill voice. "I demand justice! Justice of the king! Justice of the law! Justice to the king's aunt."

Bud looked down the room and saw Aunt Rivette struggling with some of the guards. Then she broke away from them and rushed to the throne, crying again:

"Justice, your Majesty!"

"What 's the matter with you?" asked Bud.

"Matter? Everything 's the matter with me. Are n't you the new king?"

"Then let the lord high executioner step forward!"

"Yes," said Bud. "That's what I am."

"Am I not your aunt? Am I not your aunt?"

"Yes," said Bud, again.

"Well, why am I left to live in a hut and dress in rags? Does n't the law say that every blood relation of the king shall live in a royal palace?"

"Does it?" asked Bud, turning to Tullydub.

"The law says so, your Majesty."

"And must I have that old crosspatch around me all the time?" wailed the new king.

"Crosspatch yourself!" screamed Aunt Rivette, shaking her fist at Bud. "I 'll teach you to cross-patch me when I get you alone!"

Bud shuddered. Then he turned again to Tully-dub.

"The king can do what he likes, can't he?" the boy asked.

"Certainly, your Majesty."

"Then let the lord high executioner step forward!"

"Oh, Bud! What are you going to do?" said Fluff, seizing him tightly by the arm.

"You let me alone!" answered Bud. "I 'm not going to be a king for nothing. And Aunt Rivette whipped me once — sixteen hard switches! I counted 'em."

The executioner was now bowing before him.

"Get a switch," commanded the king.

The executioner brought a long, slender birch bough.

"Now," said Bud, "you give Aunt Rivette sixteen

good switches."

"Oh, don't! Don't, Bud!" pleaded Meg.

Aunt Rivette fell on her knees, pale and trembling. In agony she raised her hands.

"I 'll never do it again! Let me off, your Majesty!" she screamed. "Let me off this once! I 'll never do it again! Never! Never!"

"All right," said Bud, with a cheery smile. "I 'll let you off this time. But if you don't behave, or if you interfere with me or Fluff, I 'll have the lord high executioner take charge of you. Just remember I 'm the king, and then we 'll get along all right. Now you may go upstairs if you wish to and pick out a room on the top story. Fluff and I are going to play."

With this he laid his crown carefully on the seat of the throne and threw off his ermine robe.

"Come on, Fluff! We 've had enough business for to-day," he said, and dragged the laughing princess from the room, while Aunt Rivette meekly followed the lord high steward up the stairs to a comfortable apartment just underneath the roof.

She was very well satisfied at last; and very soon she sent for the lord high purse-bearer and demanded money with which to buy some fine clothes for herself.

This was given her willingly, for the law provided for the comfort of every relative of the king, and knowing this, Aunt Rivette fully intended to be the most comfortable woman in the kingdom of Noland.

Chapter VII.

THE WINGS OF AUNT RIVETTE.

Bud and Meg had plenty to occupy them in looking over and admiring their new possessions. First they went to the princess's rooms, where Fluff ordered her seven maids to spread out all the beautiful gowns she had received. And forty of them made quite an imposing show, I assure you. They were all dainty and sweet and of rich material, suitable for all occasions, and of all colors and shades. Of course there were none with trains, for Margaret, although a princess, was only a little girl; but the gowns were gay with bright ribbons and jeweled buttons and clasps; and each one had its hat and hosiery and slippers to match.

After admiring the dresses for a time, they looked at Bud's new clothes—twenty suits of velvets, brocades, and finely woven cloths. Some had diamonds and precious gems sewn on them for ornaments, while others were plain; but the poorest suit there was finer than the boy had ever dreamed of possessing.

There were also many articles of apparel to go with these suits, such as shoes with diamond buckles, silken stockings, neck laces, and fine linen; and there was a beautiful little sword, with a gold scabbard and a jeweled hilt, that the little king could wear on state occasions.

However, when the children had examined the gowns and suits to their satisfaction, they began looking for other amusement.

After admiring the dresses, they looked at Bud's new clothes.

"Do you know, Fluff," said the boy, "there is n't a single toy or plaything in this whole palace?"

"I suppose the old king did n't care for playthings," replied Fluff, thoughtfully.

Just then there was a knock at the door, and Aunt

Rivette came hobbling into the room. Her wrinkled old face was full of eagerness, and in her hands she clasped the purse of golden coins the lord high purse-bearer had given her.

"See what I 've got!" she cried, holding out the purse. "And I 'm going to buy the finest clothes in all the kingdom! And ride in the king's carriage! And have a man to wait upon me! And make Mammy Skib and Mistress Kappleson and all the other neighbors wild with jealousy!"

"I don't care," said Bud.

"Why, you owe everything to me!" cried Aunt Rivette. "If I had n't brought you to Nole on the donkey's back, you would n't have been the forty-seventh person to enter the gate."

"That 's true," said Meg.

But Bud was angry.

"I know it 's true," he said; "but look here, you must n't bother us. Just keep out of our way, please, and let me alone, and then I won't care how many new dresses you buy."

"I 'm going to spend every piece of this gold!" she exclaimed, clasping the purse with her wrinkled hands. "But I don't like to go through the streets in this poor dress. Won't you lend me your cloak, Meg, until I get back?"

"Of course I will," returned the girl; and going to the closet, she brought out the magic cloak the fairy had given her and threw it over Aunt Rivette's

*Almost before she knew it, Aunt Rivette had descended
to the roof of the royal stables.*

shoulders. For she was sorry for the old woman, and this was the prettiest cloak she had.

So old Rivette, feeling very proud and anxious to spend her money, left the palace and walked as fast as her tottering legs would carry her down the street in the direction of the shops. "I 'll buy a yellow silk," she mumbled to herself, half aloud, "and a white velvet, and a purple brocade, and a sky-blue bonnet with crimson plumes! And won't the neighbors stare then? Oh, dear! If I could only walk faster! And the shops are so far! I wish I could fly!"

Now she was wearing the magic cloak when she expressed this wish, and no sooner had she spoken than two great feathery wings appeared, fastened to her shoulders.

The old woman stopped short, turned her head, and saw the wings; and then she gave a scream and a jump and began waving her arms frantically.

The wings flopped at the same time, raising her slowly from the ground, and she began to soar gracefully above the heads of the astonished people, who thronged the streets below.

"Stop! Help! Murder!" shrieked Rivette, kicking her feet in great agitation, and at the same time flopping nervously her new wings. "Save me, some one! Save me!"

"Why don't you save yourself?" asked a man

below. "Stop flying, if you want to reach the earth again!"

This struck old Rivette as a sensible suggestion. She was quite a distance in the air by this time; but she tried to hold her wings steady and not flop them, and the result was that she began to float slowly downward. Then, with horror, she saw she was sinking directly upon the branches of a prickly-pear tree; so she screamed and began flying again, and the swift movement of her wings sent her high into the air.

So great was her terror that she nearly fainted; but she shut her eyes so that she might not see how high up she was, and held her wings rigid and began gracefully to float downward again.

By and by she opened her eyes and found one of her sleeves was just missing the sharp point of a lightning-rod on a tower of the palace. So she began struggling and flopping anew, and, almost before she knew it, Aunt Rivette had descended to the roof of the royal stables. Here she sat down and began to weep and wail, while a great crowd gathered below and watched her.

"Get a ladder! *Please* get a ladder!" begged old Rivette. "If you don't, I shall fall and break my neck."

By this time Bud and Fluff had come out to see what caused the excitement; and, to their amazement, they found their old aunt perched high up on the stable roof, with two great wings growing out from her back.

For a moment they could not understand what had happened. Then Margaret cried:

"Oh, Bud, I let her wear the magic cloak! She must have made a wish!"

"Help! Get a ladder!"
wailed the old woman.

"Help! Help! Get a ladder!" wailed the old woman, catching sight of her nephew and niece.

"Well, you *are* a bird, Aunt Rivette!" shouted Bud, gleefully, for he was in a teasing mood. "You don't need a ladder! I don't see why you can't fly down the same way you flew up." And all the people shouted: "Yes, yes! The king is right! Fly down!"

Just then Rivette's feet began to slip on the sloping roof; so she made a wild struggle to save herself, and the result was that she fluttered her wings in just exactly the right way to sink down gradually to the ground.

"You 'll be all right as soon as you know how to

"Why, Aunt Rivette, I do believe you must be the only person in all the world who can fly!"

use your wings," said Bud, with a laugh. "But where did you get 'em, anyhow?"

"I don't know," said Aunt Rivette, much relieved to be on earth again, and rather pleased to have attracted so much attention. "Are the wings pretty?"

"They are perfectly lovely!" cried Fluff, clapping

her hands in glee. "Why, Aunt Rivette, I do believe you must be the only person in all the world who can fly!"

"But I think you look like an overgrown buzzard," said Bud.

Now it happened that all this praise, and the wondering looks of the people, did a great deal to reconcile Rivette to her new wings. Indeed, she began to feel a certain pride and distinction in them; and, finding she had through all the excitement retained her grasp on the purse of gold, she now wrapped the magic cloak around her and walked away to the shops, followed by a crowd of men, women, and children.

CHAPTER VIII.

THE ROYAL RECEPTION.

As for the king and Princess Fluff, they returned to the palace and dressed themselves in some of their prettiest garments, telling Jikki to have two ponies saddled and ready for them to ride upon.

"We really *must* have some toys," said Meg, with decision; "and now that we are rich, there is no reason why we can't buy what we want."

"That 's true," answered Bud. "The old king had n't anything to play with. Poor old man! I wonder what he did to amuse himself."

They mounted their ponies, and, followed by the chief counselor and the lord high purse-bearer in one of the state carriages, and a guard of soldiers for escort, they rode down the streets of the city on a pleasure-jaunt, amid the shouts of the loyal populace.

By and by Bud saw a toy-shop in one of the streets, and he and Fluff slipped down from their ponies and went inside to examine the toys. It was a well-stocked shop, and there were rows upon rows of beautiful dolls on the shelves, which attracted Margaret's attention at once.

"Oh, Bud," she exclaimed, "I must have one of

these dollies!"

"Take your choice," said her brother, calmly, although his own heart was beating with delight at the sight of all the toys arranged before him.

"I don't know which to choose," sighed the little

F RICHARDSON

"We'll take 'em all," declared Bud.

princess, looking from one doll to another with long-ing and indecision.

"We 'll take 'em all," declared Bud.

"All! What—all these rows of dollies?" she gasped.

"Why not?" asked the king. Then he turned to the men who kept the shop and said:

"Call in that old fellow who carries the money."

When the lord high purse-bearer appeared, Bud said to him:

"Pay the man for all these dolls; and for this— and this—and this—and this!" and he began picking out the prettiest toys in all the shop, in the most reckless way you can imagine.

The soldiers loaded the carriage down with Meg's dolls, and a big cart was filled with Bud's toys. Then the purse-bearer paid the bill, although he sighed deeply several times while counting out the money. But the new king paid no attention to old Tillydib; and when the treasures were all secured the children mounted their ponies and rode joyfully back to the palace, followed in a procession by the carriage filled with dolls, and the cart loaded with toys, while Tullydub and Tillydib, being unable to ride in the carriage, trotted along at the rear on foot.

Bud had the toys and dolls all carried upstairs into a big room, and then he ordered everybody to keep out while he and Fluff arranged their playthings around the room and upon the tables and chairs, besides littering the floor so that they could hardly find a clear place large enough for some of their romping games.

"After all," he said to his sister, "it's a good thing to be a king!"

"Or even a princess," added Meg, busily dressing and arranging her dolls.

They made Jikki bring their dinner to them in the

"play-room," as Bud called it; but neither of the children could spare much time to eat, their treasures being all so new and delightful.

Soon after dusk, while Jikki was lighting the candles, the chief counselor came to the door to say that the king must be ready to attend the royal reception in five minutes.

"I won't," said Bud. "I just won't."

"But you *must*, your Majesty!" declared old Tullydub.

"Am I not the king?" demanded Bud, looking up from where he was arranging an army of wooden soldiers.

"Certainly, your Majesty," was the reply.

"And is n't the king's will the law?" continued Bud.

"Certainly, your Majesty!"

"Well, if that is so, just understand that I won't come. Go away and let me alone!"

"But the people expect your Majesty to attend the royal reception," protested old Tullydub, greatly astonished. "It is the usual custom, you know; and they would be greatly disappointed if your Majesty did not appear."

"I don't care," said Bud. "You get out of here and let me alone!"

"But, your Majesty—"

The king threw a toy cannon at his chief counselor, and the old man ducked to escape it, and then quickly closed the door.

"Bud," said the princess, softly, "you were just say-ing it's great fun to be a king."

"So it is," he answered promptly.

"But father used to tell us," continued the girl, try-ing a red hat on a brown-haired doll, "that people

F. RICHARDSON
The king threw a toy cannon at his chief counselor.

in this world always have to pay for any good thing they get."

"What do you mean?" said Bud, with surprise.

"I mean if you're going to be the king, and wear fine clothes, and eat lovely dinners, and live in a pal-ace, and have countless servants, and all the playthings you want, and your own way in everything and with everybody—then you ought to be willing to pay for all these pleasures."

"How? But how *can* I pay for them?" demanded Bud, staring at her.

"By attending the royal receptions, and doing all the disagreeable things the king is expected to do," she answered.

Bud thought about it for a minute. Then he got up, walked over to his sister, and kissed her.

"I b'lieve you 're right, Fluff," he said, with a sigh. "I 'll go to that reception to-night, and take it as I would take a dose of medicine."

"Of course you will!" returned Fluff, looking up at him brightly; "and I 'll go with you! The dolls can wait till to-morrow. Have Jikki brush your hair, and I 'll get my maids to dress me!"

Old Tullydub was wondering how he might best explain the king's absence to the throng of courtiers gathered to attend the royal reception, when, to his surprise and relief, his Majesty entered the room, accompanied by the Princess Fluff. The king wore a velvet suit trimmed with gold lace, and at his side hung the beautiful jeweled sword. Meg was dressed in a soft white silken gown, and looked as sweet and fair as a lily.

The courtiers and their ladies, who were all wearing their most handsome and becoming apparel, received their little king with great respect, and several of the wealthiest and most noble among them came up to Bud to converse with him.

But the king did not know what to say to these great personages, and so the royal reception began to be a very stupid affair.

Fluff saw that all the people were standing in stiff rows and looking at one another uneasily, so she went to Bud and whispered to him.

"Is there a band of musicians in the palace?" the king inquired of Tellydeb, who stood near.

"Yes, your Majesty."

"Send for them, then," commanded Bud.

Presently the musicians appeared, and the king ordered them to play a waltz. But the chief counselor rushed up and exclaimed:

"Oh, your Majesty! This is against all rule and custom!"

"Silence!" said Bud, angrily. "*I 'll* make the rules and customs in this kingdom hereafter. We 're going to have a dance."

"But it 's so dreadful—so unconventional, your Majesty! It 's so—what shall I call it?"

"Here! I 've had enough of this," declared Bud. "You go and stand in that corner, with your face to the wall, till I tell you to sit down," he added, remembering a time when his father, the ferryman, had inflicted a like punishment upon him.

Somewhat to his surprise, Tullydub at once obeyed the command, and then Bud made his first speech to the people.

"We 're going to have a dance," he said; "so pitch in and have a good time. If there 's anything you want, ask for it. You 're all welcome to stay as long as you please and go home when you get ready."

This seemed to please the company, for every one applauded the king's speech. Then the musicians began to play, and the people were soon dancing and enjoying themselves greatly.

Princess Fluff had a good many partners that evening, but Bud did not care to dance—he preferred to look on; and, after a time, he brought old Tullydub out of his corner, and made the chief counselor promise to be good and not annoy him again.

"But it is my duty to counsel the king," protested the old man, solemnly.

"When I want your advice I 'll ask for it," said Bud.

While Tullydub stood beside the throne, looking somewhat sulky and disagreeable, the door opened and Aunt Rivette entered the reception-room. She was clothed in a handsome gown of bright-green velvet, trimmed with red and yellow flowers, and the wings stuck out from the folds at her back in a way that was truly wonderful.

Aunt Rivette seemed in an amiable mood. She smiled and curtsied to all the people, who stopped dancing to stare at her, and she even fluttered her wings once or twice to show that she was proud of being unlike all the others present.

*One screamed "Murder!"
and the other "Help!"*

Bud had to laugh at her, she looked so funny; and then a mischievous thought came to him, and he commanded old Tullydub to dance with her.

"But I don't dance, your Majesty!" exclaimed the

horrified chief counselor.

"Try it; I 'm sure you can dance," returned Bud. "If you don't know how, it 's time you learned."

So the poor man was forced to place his arm about Aunt Rivette's waist and to whirl her around in a waltz. The old woman knew as little about dancing as did Tullydub, and they were exceedingly awkward, bumping into every one they came near. Presently Aunt Rivette's feet slipped, and she would have tumbled upon the floor with the chief counselor had she not begun to flutter her wings wildly.

So, instead of falling, she rose gradually into the air, carrying Tullydub with her; for they clung to each other in terror, and one screamed "Murder!" and the other "Help!" in their loudest voices.

Bud laughed until the tears stood in his eyes; but Aunt Rivette, after bumping both her own head and that of the chief counselor against the ceiling several times, finally managed to control the action of her wings and to descend to the floor again.

As soon as he was released, old Tullydub fled from the room; and Aunt Rivette, vowing she would dance no more, seated herself beside Bud and watched the revel until nearly midnight, when the courtiers and their ladies dispersed to their own homes, declaring that they had never enjoyed a more delightful evening.

Chapter IX.

NEXT morning Aunt Rivette summoned Jikki to her room, and said:

"Take these shoes and clean and polish them; and carry down this tray of breakfast dishes; and send this hat to the milliner to have the feathers curled; and return this cloak to the Princess Fluff, with my compliments, and say I 'm much obliged for the loan of it."

Poor Jikki hardly knew how to manage so many orders. He took the shoes in his left hand, and the tray of dishes he balanced upon the other upraised palm. But the hat and cloak were too many for him. So Aunt Rivette, calling him "a stupid idiot,"— probably because he had no more hands,—set the plumed hat upon Jikki's head and spread the cloak over his shoulders, and ordered him to make haste away.

Jikki was glad enough to go, for the fluttering of Aunt Rivette's wings made him nervous; but he had to descend the stairs cautiously, for the hat was tipped nearly over his eyes, and if he stumbled he would be sure to spill the tray of dishes.

He reached the first landing of the broad stairs in

safety, but at the second landing the hat joggled forward so that he could see nothing at all, and one of
the shoes dropped from his hand.

"Dear me!" sighed the old man; "I wonder what
I shall do now? If I pick up the shoe I shall drop

Jikki had to descend the stairs cautiously.

the dishes; and I can't set down this tray because
I 'm blinded by this terrible hat! Dear—dear! If
I 'm to be at the beck and call of that old woman, and
serve the new king at the same time, I shall have my
hands full. My hands, in fact, are full now. I really
wish I had half a dozen servants to wait on *me !*"

Jikki knew nothing at all about the magic power of the cloak that fell from his shoulders; so his astonishment was profound when some one seized the shoe from his left hand and some one else removed the tray from his right hand, and still another person snatched the plumed hat from his head.

But then he saw, bowing and smirking before him, six young men, who looked as much alike as peas in the same pod, and all of whom wore very neat and handsome liveries of wine-color, with silver buttons on their coats.

Jikki blinked and stared at these people, and rubbed his eyes to make sure he was awake.

"Who are you?" he managed to ask.

"We are your half a dozen servants, sir," answered the young men, speaking all together and bowing again.

Jikki gasped and raised his hands with sudden amazement as he gazed in wonder upon the row of six smart servants.

"But—what—are you doing here?" he stammered.

"We are here to wait upon you, sir, as is our duty," they answered respectfully.

Jikki rubbed his left ear, as was his custom when perplexed; and then he thought it all over. And the more he thought the more perplexed he became.

"I don't understand!" he finally said, in a weak voice.

F. RICHARDSON

"You wished for us, and

"You wished for us, and here we are," declared the six, once more bowing low before him.

"I know," said Jikki. "But I 've often wished for many other things—and never got a single one of the wishes before!"

The young men did not attempt to explain this curious fact. They stood in a straight row before their master, as if awaiting his orders. One held the shoe Jikki had dropped, another its mate, still another the plumed hat, and a fourth the tray of dishes.

"You see," remarked Jikki, shaking his head sadly at the six, "I 'm only a servant myself."

"You are our master, sir!" announced the young men, their voices blended into one.

here we are," declared the six.

"I wish," said Jikki, solemnly, "you were all back where you came from!" And then he paused to see if this wish also would be fulfilled. But no; the magic cloak conferred the fulfilment of but one wish upon its wearer, and the half a dozen servants remained standing rigidly before him.

Jikki arose with a sigh.

"Come downstairs to my private room," he said, "and we 'll talk the matter over."

So they descended the grand stairway to the main hall of the grand palace, Jikki going first and his servants following at a respectful distance. Just off the hall Jikki had a pleasant room where he could sit when not employed, and into this he led the six.

After all, he considered, it would not be a bad thing to have half a dozen servants; they would save his old legs from many a tiresome errand. But just as they reached the hall a new thought struck him, and he turned suddenly upon his followers:

"See here!" he exclaimed. "How much wages do you fellows expect?"

"We expect no wages at all, sir," they answered.

"What! nothing at all!" Jikki was so startled that he scarcely had strength remaining to stagger into his private room and sink into a chair.

"No wages! Six servants, and no wages to pay!" he muttered. "Why, it 's wonderful—marvelous—astounding!"

Then he thought to himself: "I 'll try 'em, and see if they 'll really work." And aloud he asked:

"How can I tell you apart—one from another?"

Each servant raised his right arm and pointed to a silver badge upon his left breast; and then Jikki discovered that they were all numbered, from "one" up to "six."

"Ah! very good!" said Jikki. "Now, number six, take this shoe into the boot-room, and clean and polish it."

Number six bowed and glided from the room as swiftly and silently as if he were obeying a command of the King of Noland.

"Number five," continued Jikki, "take this tray to the kitchen." Number five obeyed instantly, and Jikki chuckled with delight.

"Number two, take this to the milliner in Royal Street, and have the feathers curled."

Number two bowed and departed almost before the words had left Jikki's mouth; and then the king's valet regarded the remaining three in some perplexity.

"Half a dozen servants is almost too many," he thought. "It will keep me busy to keep them busy. I should have wished for only one—or two at the most."

Just then he remembered something.

"Number four," said he, "go after number two and tell the milliner that the hat belongs to Madam Rivette, the king's aunt."

And a few moments later, when the remaining two servants, standing upright before him, had begun to make him nervous, Jikki cried out:

"Number three, take this other shoe down to the boot-room and tell number six to clean and polish it also."

This left but one of the six unoccupied, and Jikki was wondering what to do with him when a bell rang.

"That's the king's bell," said Jikki.

"I am not the king's servant; I am here only to wait upon you," said number one, without moving to answer the bell.

"Then I must go myself," sighed the valet, and

rushed away to obey the king's summons.

Scarcely had he disappeared when Tollydob, the lord high general, entered the room and said in a gruff voice:

"Where is Jikki? Where's that rascal Jikki?"

Number one, standing stiffly at one end of the room, made no reply.

"Answer me, you scoundrel!" roared the old general. "Where's Jikki?"

Still number one stood silent, and this so enraged old Tollydob that he raised his cane and aimed a furious blow at the young man. The cane seemed to pass directly through the fellow, and. it struck the wall behind so forcibly that it split into two parts.

This amazed Tollydob. He stared a moment at the silent servant, and then turned his back upon him and sat down in Jikki's chair. Here his eyes fell upon the magic cloak, which the king's valet had thrown down.

Tollydob, attracted by the gorgeous coloring and soft texture of the garment, picked up the cloak and threw it over his shoulders; and then he walked to a mirror and began admiring his reflection.

While thus engaged, Jikki returned, and the valet was so startled at seeing the lord high general that he never noticed the cloak at all.

"His Majesty has asked to see your Highness," said Jikki; "and I was about to go in search of you."

"I 'll go to the king at once," answered Tollydob, and as he walked away Jikki suddenly noticed that he was wearing the cloak. "Oho!" thought the valet, "he has gone off with the Princess Fluff's pretty cloak; but when he returns from the king's chamber I 'll get it again and send number one to carry it to its rightful owner."

Jikki.

Chapter X.

THE COUNSELORS WEAR THE MAGIC CLOAK.

WHEN Tollydob, still wearing the magic cloak, had bowed before the king, Bud asked:

"How many men are there in the royal army, general?"

"Seven thousand seven hundred and seventy-seven, may it please your gracious Majesty," returned Tollydob—"that is, without counting myself."

"And do they obey your orders promptly?" inquired Bud, who felt a little doubt on this point.

"Yes, indeed!" answered the general, proudly. "They are terribly afraid of my anger."

"And yet you 're a very small man to command so large an army," said the king.

The lord high general flushed with shame; for, although he was both old and fat, he was so short of stature that he stood but a trifle taller than Bud himself. And, like all short men, he was very sensitive about his height.

"I 'm a terrible fighter, your Majesty," declared Tollydob, earnestly; "and when I 'm on horseback my small size is little noticed. Nevertheless," he added, with a sigh, "it is a good thing to be tall. I wish I were ten feet high."

No sooner were the words spoken than Bud gave a cry of astonishment; for the general's head shot suddenly upward until his gorgeous hat struck the

"I wish I were ten feet high."

ceiling and was jammed down tightly over the startled man's eyes and nose.

The room was just ten feet high, and Tollydob was now ten feet tall; but for a time the old general could not think what had happened to him, and Bud, observing for the first time that Tollydob wore the magic cloak, began to shriek with laughter at the comical result of the old man's wish.

Hearing the king laugh, the general tore the hat from his head and looked at himself in mingled terror and admiration.

From being a very small man he had suddenly become a giant, and the change was so great that Tollydob might well be amazed.

"What has happened, your Majesty?" he asked in a trembling voice.

"Why, don't you see, you were wearing my sister's magic cloak," said Bud, still laughing at the big man's woeful face; "and it grants to every wearer the fulfilment of one wish."

"Only one?" inquired poor Tollydob. "I'd like to be a little smaller, I confess."

"It can't be helped now," said Bud. "You wished to be ten feet tall, and there you are! And there you'll have to stay, Tollydob, whether you like it or not. But I'm very proud of you. You must be the greatest general in all the world, you know!"

Tollydob brightened up at this, and tried to sit down in a chair: but it crushed to pieces under his weight; so he sighed and remained standing. Then he threw the magic cloak upon the floor, with a little shudder at its fairy powers, and said:

"If I'd only known, I might have become just six feet tall instead of ten!"

"Never mind," said Bud, consolingly. "If we ever

have a war, you will strike terror into the ranks of the enemy, and every one in Noland will admire you immensely. Hereafter you will be not only the lord high general, but the lord *very* high general."

So Tollydob went away to show himself to the chief counselor; and he had to stoop very low to pass through the doorway.

When Jikki saw the gigantic man coming out of the king's chamber, he gave a scream and fled in terror; and, strange to say, this effect was very agreeable to the lord high general, who loved to make people fear him.

Bud ran to tell Fluff of the curious thing that had happened to his general; and so it was that when the lord high executioner entered the palace there was no one around to receive him. He made his way into the king's chamber, and there he found the magic cloak lying upon the floor.

" I 've seen the Princess Fluff wearing this," thought the lord high executioner; "so it must belong to her. I 'll take it to her rooms, for it is far too pretty to be lying around in this careless way, and Jikki ought to be scolded for allowing it."

So Tellydeb picked up the cloak and laid it over his arm; then he admired the bright hues that ran through the fabric, and presently his curiosity got the better of him; he decided to try it on and see how he would look in it.

While thus employed the sound of a girl's sweet

laughter fell upon Tellydeb's ears, seeming to come from a far distance.

"The princess must be in the royal gardens," he said to himself. "I 'll go there and find her."

So the lord high executioner walked through the great hall, still wearing the cloak, and finally came to the back of the palace and passed a doorway leading into the gardens. All was quiet here, save for the song of the birds as they fluttered among the trees; but at the other end of the garden Tellydeb caught a glimpse of a white gown, which he suspected might be that of the little princess.

He walked along the paths slowly, enjoying the scent of the flowers and the peacefulness of the scene; for the lord high executioner was a gentle-natured man and delighted in beautiful sights.

After a time he reached a fruit-orchard, and saw hanging far up in a big tree a fine red apple. Tellydeb paused and looked at this longingly.

"I wish I could reach that apple!" he said, with a sigh, as he extended his arm upward.

Instantly the arm stretched toward the apple, which was at least forty feet away from the lord high executioner; and while the astonished man eyed his elongated arm in surprise, the hand clutched the apple, plucked it, and drew it back to him; and there he stood—the apple in his hand, and his arm apparently the same as it had been before he accomplished the wonderful feat.

For a moment the counselor was overcome with fear. The cloak dropped unnoticed from his shoulders and fell upon the graveled walk, while Tellydeb sank upon a bench and shivered.

"I wish I could reach that apple!" he said, with a sigh, as he extended his arm upward.

"It—it was like magic!" he murmured. "I but reached out my hand—so—it went nearly to the top of the tree, and—"

Here he gave a cry of wonder, for again his arm stretched the distance and touched the topmost branches of the tree. He drew it back hastily, and turned to see if any one had observed him. But this part of the garden was deserted, so the old man eagerly tested his new accomplishment.

He plucked a rose from a bush a dozen yards to the right, and having smelled its odor he placed it in a vase that stood twenty feet to his left. Then he noted a fountain far across a hedge, and reaching the distance easily, dipped his hand in the splashing water. It was all very amazing, this sudden power to reach a great distance, and the lord high executioner was so pleased with the faculty that when he discovered old Jikki standing in the palace doorway, he laughingly fetched him a box on the ear that sent the valet scampering away to his room in amazed terror.

Said Tellydeb to himself: " Now I 'll go home and show my wife what a surprising gift I have acquired."

So he left the garden; and not long afterward old Tallydab, the lord high steward, came walking down the path, followed by his little dog Ruffles. I am not certain whether it was because his coat was so shaggy or his temper so uncertain that Tallydab's dog was named Ruffles; but the name fitted well both the looks and the disposition of the tiny animal. Nevertheless, the lord high steward was very fond of his dog, which followed him everywhere except to the king's council-chamber; and often the old man would tell Ruffles his troubles and worries, and talk to the dog just as one would to a person.

To-day, as they came slowly down the garden-walk, Tallydab noticed a splendid cloak lying upon the path.

"How very beautiful!" he exclaimed, as he stooped to pick it up. "I have never seen anything like this since the Princess Fluff first rode into Nole beside her brother the king. Isn't it a lovely cloak, Ruffles?"

The dog gave a subdued yelp and wagged his stubby tail.

"How do I look in it, Ruffles?" continued the lord high steward, wrapping the folds of the magic cloak about him; "how do I look in such gorgeous apparel?"

The dog stopped wagging its tail and looked up at its master earnestly.

"How do I look?" again said Tallydab. "I declare, I wish you could talk!"

"You look perfectly ridiculous," replied the dog, in a rather harsh voice.

The lord high steward jumped nearly three feet in the air, so startled was he by Ruffles's reply. Then he bent down, a hand on each knee, and regarded the dog curiously.

"I thought, at first, you had spoken!" said he.

"What caused you to change your mind?" asked Ruffles, peevishly. "I *did* speak— I *am* speaking. Can't you believe it?"

The lord high steward drew a deep sigh of conviction.

"I believe it!" he made answer. "I have always declared you were a wonderful dog, and now you prove I am right. Why, you are the only dog I ever

"You look perfectly ridiculous!" replied the dog.

heard of who could talk!"

"Except in fairy tales," said Ruffles, calmly, "Don't forget the fairy tales."

"I don't forget," replied Tallydab. "But this is n't a fairy tale, Ruffles. It 's real life in the kingdom of Noland."

"To be sure," answered Ruffles. "But see here, my dear master: now that I am, at last, able to talk, please allow me to ask you for something decent to eat. I 'd like a good meal for once, just to see what it is like."

"A good meal!" exclaimed the steward. "Why, my friend, don't I give you a big bone every day?"

"You do," said the dog; "and I nearly break my teeth on it, trying to crack it to get a little marrow. Whatever induces people to give their dogs bones instead of meat?"

"Why, I thought you liked bones!" protested Tally-dab, sitting on the bench and looking at his dog in astonishment.

"Well, I don't. I prefer something to eat—something good and wholesome, such as you eat yourself," growled Ruffles.

The lord high steward gave a laugh.

"Why," said he, "don't you remember that old Mother Hubbard

"Ah! that *was* a fairy tale," interrupted Ruffles, impatiently. "And there was n't even a bone in her cupboard, after all. Don't mention Mother Hubbard to me, if you want to retain my friendship."

"And that reminds me," resumed the steward with a scowl, "that a few minutes ago you said I looked ridiculous in this lovely cloak."

"You do!" said Ruffles, with a sniff.   "It is a girl's cloak, and not fit for a wrinkled old man like you."

F. RICHARDSON

"Why, I thought you liked bones!" protested Tallydab.

"I believe you are right," answered Tallydab, with a sigh; and he removed the cloak from his shoulders and hung it over the back of the garden seat. "In regard to the meat that you so long for," he added, "if you will follow me to the royal kitchen I will see that you have all you desire."

"Spoken like a good friend!" exclaimed the dog.

"Let us go at once."

So they passed down the garden to the kitchen door, and the magic cloak, which had wrought such wonderful things that day, still remained neglectfully cast aside.

It was growing dusk when old Tillydib, the lord high purse-bearer, stole into the garden and sat upon the bench to smoke his pipe in peace. All the afternoon he had been worried by people with bills for this thing or that, and the royal purse was very light indeed when Tillydib had at last managed to escape to the garden.

"If this keeps up," he reflected, "there will be no money left; and then I 'm sure I don't know what will become of us all!"

The air was chilly. The old counselor shivered a little, and noting the cloak that lay over the back of the seat, drew it about his shoulders.

"It will be five months," he muttered half aloud, "before we can tax the people for more money; and before five months are up the king and his counselors may all starve to death — even in this splendid palace! Heigh-ho! I wish the royal purse would always remain full, no matter how much money I drew from it!"

The big purse, which had lain lightly on his knee, now slid off and pulled heavily upon the golden chain which the old man wore around his neck to fasten the purse to him securely.

Aroused from his anxious thoughts, Tillydib lifted
the purse to his lap again, and was astonished to feel
its weight.   He opened the clasp and saw that the
huge sack was actually running over with gold
pieces.

"Now, where on earth did all this wealth come

F. RICHARDSON

"I wish the royal purse would always remain full."

from?" he exclaimed, shaking his head in a puzzled
way.   " I'll go at once and pay some of the creditors
who are waiting for me."

So he ran to the royal treasury, which was a front
room in the palace, and began paying every one who
presented an account.   He expected presently to
empty the purse; but no matter how heavily he drew

upon the contents, it remained ever as full as in the beginning.

"It must be," thought the old man, when the last bill had been paid, "that my idle wish has in some mysterious way been granted."

But he did not know he owed his good fortune to the magic cloak, which he still wore.

As he was leaving the room, he met the king and Princess Fluff, who were just come from dinner; and the girl exclaimed:

"Why, there is my cloak! Where did you get it, Tillydib?"

"I found it in the garden," answered the lord high purse-bearer; "but take it, if it is yours. And here is something to repay you for the loan of it;" and he poured into her hands a heap of glittering gold.

"Oh, thank you!" cried Fluff; and taking the precious cloak she dropped the gold into it and carried it to her room.

"I 'll never lend it again unless it is really necessary," she said to herself. "It was very careless of Aunt Rivette to leave my fairy cloak in the garden."

And then after carefully folding it and wrapping it up she locked it in a drawer, and hid the key where no one but herself could find it.

Chapter XI.

THE WITCH-QUEEN.

It is not very far from the kingdom of Noland to the kingdom of Ix. If you followed the steps of Quavo the minstrel, you would climb the sides of a steep mountain-range, and go down on the other side, and cross a broad and swift river, and pick your way through a dark forest. You would then have reached the land of Ix and would find an easy path into the big city.

But even before one came to the city he would see the high marble towers of Queen Zixi's magnificent palace, and pause to wonder at its beauty

Quavo the minstrel had been playing his harp in the city of Nole, and his eyes were sharp; so he had seen many things to gossip and sing about, and therefore never doubted he would be warmly welcomed by Queen Zixi.

He reached the marble palace about dusk, one evening, and was bidden to the feast which was about to be served.

A long table ran down the length of the lofty hall built in the center of the palace; and this table was covered with gold and silver platters bearing many kinds of meats and fruits and vegetables, while tall, ornamented stands contained sweets and delicacies to tickle the palate.

At the head of the table, on a jeweled throne, sat Queen Zixi herself, a vision of radiant beauty and charming grace.

Her hair was yellow as spun gold, and her wondrous eyes raven black in hue. Her skin was fair as a lily, save where her cheek was faintly tinted with a flush of rose-color.

Dainty and lovely, indeed, was the Queen of Ix in appearance; yet none of her lords or attendants cast more than a passing glance upon her beauty. For they were used to seeing her thus.

There were graybeards at her table this evening who could remember the queen's rare beauty since they were boys; ay, and who had been told by their fathers and grandfathers of Queen Zixi's loveliness when they also were mere children. In fact, no one in Ix had ever heard of the time when the land was not ruled by this same queen, or when she was not in appearance as young and fair as she was to-day. Which easily proves she was not an ordinary person at all.

And I may as well tell you here that Queen Zixi, despite the fact that she looked to be no more than sixteen, was in reality six hundred and eighty-three years of age, and had prolonged her life in this extraordinary way by means of the arts of witchcraft.

I do not mean by this that she was an evil person. She had always ruled her kingdom wisely and liberally, and the people of Ix made no manner of complaint against their queen. If there were a war, she

This was the moment Quavo had eagerly awaited.

led her armies in person, clad in golden mail and helmet; and in years of peace she taught them to sow and reap grain, and to fashion many useful articles of metal, and to build strong and substantial houses. Nor were her taxes ever more than the people could bear.

Yet, for all this, Zixi was more feared than loved; for every one remembered she was a witch, and also knew she was hundreds of years old. So, no matter how amiable their queen might be, she was always treated with extreme respect, and folks weighed well their words when they conversed with her.

Next the queen, on both sides of the table, sat her most favored nobles and their ladies; farther down were the rich merchants and officers of the army; and at the lower end were servants and members of the household. For this was the custom in the land of Ix.

Quavo the harpist sat near the lower end; and, when all had been comfortably fed, the queen called upon him for a song. This was the moment Quavo had eagerly awaited. He took his harp, seated himself in a niche of the wall, and, according to the manner of ancient minstrels, he sang of the things he had seen in other lands, thus serving his hearers with the news of the day as well as pleasing them with his music. This is the way he began:

> "Of Noland now a tale I 'll sing,
> Where reigns a strangely youthful king—
> A boy, who has by chance alone
> Been called to sit upon a throne.
> His sister shares his luck, and she
> The fairies' friend is said to be;
> For they did mystic arts invoke
> And weave for her a magic cloak
> Which grants its wearer—thus I 'm told—
> Gifts more precious far than gold.

"She 's but to wish, and her desire
Quite instantly she will acquire;
And when she lends it to her friends,
The favor unto them extends.

"For one who wears the cloak can fly
Like any eagle in the sky.
And one did wish, by sudden freak,
His dog be granted power to speak;
And now the beast can talk as well
As I, and also read and spell.
And —"

"Stop!" cried the queen, with sudden excitement.

"Stop!" cried the queen, with sudden excitement. "Do you lie, minstrel, or are you speaking the truth?"

Secretly glad that his news was received thus eagerly, Quavo continued to twang the harp as he replied in verse:

"Now may I die at break of day,
If false is any word I say."

"And what is this cloak like—and who owns it?" demanded the queen, impetuously.

She made a solemn vow that she would secure the magic cloak within a year.

Sang the minstrel:

> "The cloak belongs to Princess Fluff;
> 'T is woven of some secret stuff
> Which makes it gleam with splendor bright
> That fills beholders with delight."

Thereafter the beautiful Zixi remained lost in

thought, her dainty chin resting within the hollow of her hand and her eyes dreamily fixed upon the minstrel.

And Quavo, judging that his news had brought him into rare favor, told more and more wonderful tales of the magic cloak, some of which were true, while others were mere inventions of his own; for newsmongers, as every one knows, were ever unable to stick to facts since the world began.

All the courtiers and officers and servants listened with wide eyes and parted lips to the song, marveling greatly at what they had heard. And when it was finally ended, and the evening far spent, Queen Zixi threw a golden chain to the minstrel as a reward and left the hall, attended by her maidens.

Throughout the night which followed, she tossed sleeplessly upon her bed, thinking of the magic cloak and longing to possess it. And when the morning sun rose over the horizon, she made a solemn vow that she would secure the magic cloak within a year, even if it cost her the half of her kingdom.

Now the reason for this rash vow, showing Zixi's intense desire to possess the cloak, was very peculiar. Although she had been an adept at witchcraft for more than six hundred years, and was able to retain her health and remain in appearance young and beautiful, there was one thing her art was unable to deceive, and that one thing was a mirror.

To mortal eyes Zixi was charming and attractive;

Queen Zixi left the hall, attended by her maidens.

yet her reflection in a mirror showed to her an ugly old hag, bald of head, wrinkled, with toothless gums and withered, sunken cheeks.

For this reason the queen had no mirror of any sort about the palace. Even from her own dressing-room the mirror had been banished, and she depended upon her maids and hair-dressers to make her look as lovely as possible. She knew she was beautiful in appearance to others; her maids declared it continually, and in all eyes she truly read admiration.

But Zixi wanted to admire herself; and that was impossible so long as the cold mirrors showed her reflection to be the old hag others would also have seen had not her arts of witchcraft deceived them.

Everything else a woman and a queen might desire Zixi was able to obtain by her arts. Yet the one thing she could *not* have made her very unhappy.

As I have already said, she was not a bad queen. She used her knowledge of sorcery to please her own fancy or to benefit her kingdom, but never to injure any one else. So she may be forgiven for wanting to see a beautiful girl reflected in a mirror, instead of a haggard old woman in her six hundred and eighty-fourth year.

Zixi had given up all hope of ever accomplishing her object until she heard of the magic cloak. The powers of witches are somewhat limited; but she knew that the powers of fairies are boundless. So if the magic cloak could grant any human wish, as Quavo's song had told her was the case, she would manage to secure it and would at once wish for a reflection in the mirror of the same features all others beheld—and then she would become happy and content.

Chapter XII.

ZIXI DISGUISES HERSELF.

Now, as might be expected, Queen Zixi lost no time in endeavoring to secure the magic cloak. The people of Ix were not on friendly terms with the people of Noland; so she could not visit Princess Fluff openly; and she knew it was useless to try to borrow so priceless a treasure as a cloak which had been the gift of the fairies. But one way remained to her— to steal the precious robe.

So she began her preparations by telling her people she would be absent from Ix for a month, and then she retired to her own room and mixed, by the rules of witchcraft, a black mess in a silver kettle, and boiled it until it was as thick as molasses. Of this inky mixture she swallowed two teaspoonfuls every hour for six hours, muttering an incantation each time. At the end of the six hours her golden hair had become brown and her black eyes had become blue; and this was quite sufficient to disguise the pretty queen so that no one would recognize her. Then she took off her richly embroidered queenly robes, and hung them up in a closet, putting on a simple gingham dress, a white apron, and a plain hat such as common people of her country wore.

F.RICHARDSON

Of this inky mixture she swallowed two teaspoonfuls.

When these preparations had been made, Zixi slipped out the back door of the palace and walked through the city to the forest; and, although she met many people, no one suspected that she was the queen.

It was rough walking in the forest; but she got through at last, and reached the bank of the river. Here a fisherman was found, who consented to ferry

her across in his boat; and afterward Zixi climbed
the high mountain and came down the other side into
the kingdom of Noland.

She rented a neat little cottage just at the north
gateway of the city of Nole, and by the next morning there was a sign over the doorway which announced:

MISS TRUST'S
ACADEMY OF WITCHERY
FOR YOUNG LADIES.

Then Zixi had printed on green paper a lot of
handbills which read as follows:

MISS TRUST,
A pupil of the celebrated Professor Hatrack
of Hooktown-on-the-Creek, is now located at
Woodbine Villa (North Gateway of Nole),
and is prepared to teach the young ladies of
this city the *Arts of Witchcraft* according
to the most modern and approved methods.
Terms moderate.   References required.

These handbills she hired a little boy to carry to
all the aristocratic houses in Nole, and to leave one
on each door-step.   Several were left on the different
door-steps of the palace, and one of these came to the
notice of Princess Fluff.

" How funny!" she exclaimed on reading it.   " I 'll
go, and take all my eight maids with me.   It will be
no end of fun to learn to be a witch."

Many other people in Nole applied for instruction
in " Miss Trust's Academy," but Zixi told them all
she had no vacancies.   When, however, Fluff and her

maids arrived, she welcomed them with the utmost cordiality, and consented to give them their first lesson at once.

When she had seated them in her parlor, Zixi said:

"If you wish to be a witch,
    You must speak an incantation:
    You must with deliberation
    Say: 'The when of why is which!'"

"What does that mean?" asked Fluff.

"No one knows," answered Zixi; "and therefore it is a fine incantation.   Now, all the class will please repeat after me the following words:

"Erig-a-ma-role, erig-a-ma-ree;
    Jig-ger-nut, jog-ger-nit, que-jig-ger-ee.
    Sim-mer-kin, sam-mer-kin, sem-mer-ga-roo;
    Zil-li-pop, zel-li-pop, lol-li-pop-loo!"

They tried to do this, but their tongues stumbled constantly over the syllables, and one of the maids began to laugh.

"Stop laughing, please!" cried Zixi, rapping her ruler on the table.   "This is no laughing matter, I assure you, young ladies.   The science of witchcraft is a solemn and serious study, and I cannot teach it you unless you behave."

"But what's it all about?" asked Fluff.

"I'll explain what it's about to-morrow," said Zixi, with dignity.   "Now, here are two important incantations which you must learn by heart before you come to to-morrow's lesson.   If you can speak them correctly and rapidly, and above all very distinctly, I will then allow you to perform a wonderful witchery."

F. RICHARDSON

"Now, there is one thing more," continued Zixi; "and this is very important."

She handed them each a slip of paper on which were written the incantations, as follows:

Incantation No. 1.

(To be spoken only in the presence of a black cat.)

This is that, and that is this;
Bliss is blest, and blest is bliss.
Who is that, and what is who;
Shed is shod, and shud is shoe!

Incantation No. 2.

(To be spoken when the clock strikes twelve.)

What is which, and which is what;
Pat is pet, and pit is pat;
Hid is hide, and hod is hid;
Did is deed, and done is did!

"Now, there is one thing more," continued Zixi; "and this is very important. You must each wear the handsomest and most splendid cloak you can secure when you come to me to-morrow morning."

This request made Princess Fluff thoughtful all the way home, for she at once remembered her magic cloak, and wondered if the strange Miss Trust knew she possessed it.

She asked Bud about it that night, and the young king said:

"I 'm afraid this witch-woman is some one trying to get hold of your magic cloak. I would advise you not to wear it when she is around, or, more than likely, she may steal it."

So Fluff did not wear her magic cloak the next day, but selected in its place a pretty blue cape edged with gold. When she and her maids reached the cottage, Zixi cried out angrily:

"That is not your handsomest cloak. Go home at once and get the other one!"

"I won't," said Fluff, shortly.

"You must! You must!" insisted the witch-woman. "I can teach you nothing unless you wear the other cloak."

"How did you know I had another cloak?" asked the princess, suspiciously.

"By witchcraft, perhaps," said Zixi, mildly. "If you want to be a witch you must wear it."

"I don't want to be a witch," declared Fluff. "Come, girls, come; let 's go home at once."

"Wait—wait!" implored Zixi, eagerly. "If you 'll get the cloak I will teach you the most wonderful things in the world! I will make you the most powerful witch that ever lived!"

"I don't believe you," replied Fluff; and then she marched back to the palace with all her maids.

But Zixi knew her plot had failed; so she locked up the cottage and went back again to Ix, climbing the mountain and crossing the river and threading the forest with angry thoughts and harsh words.

Yet the queen was more determined than ever to secure the magic cloak. As soon as she had reën-

"That is not your handsomest cloak."

tered her palace and by more incantations had again transformed her hair to yellow and her eyes to black and dressed herself in her royal robes, she summoned her generals and counselors and told them to make ready to war upon the kingdom of Noland.

Chapter XIII.

TULLYDUB RESCUES THE KINGDOM.

ALL soldiers love to fight; so when the army of Ix learned that they were to go to war, they rejoiced exceedingly over the news.

They polished up their swords and battle-axes, and sewed all the missing buttons on their uniforms, and mended their socks, and had their hair cut, and were ready to march as soon as the queen was ready to have them start.

King Bud of Noland had an army of seven thousand seven hundred and seventy-seven men, besides a general ten feet high; but the Queen of Ix had an army more than twice as big, and she decided to lead it in person, so that when she had conquered the city of Nole she herself could seize the precious magic cloak which she so greatly coveted.

Therefore Queen Zixi rode out at the head of her army, clad in a suit of mail, with a glittering helmet upon her head that was surmounted by a flowing white plume. And all the soldiers cheered their queen and had no doubt at all that she would win a glorious victory.

Queen Zixi rode out at the head of her army, clad in a suit of mail.

Quavo the minstrel, who wandered constantly about, was on his way to Noland again; and while Queen Zixi's army was cutting a path through the forest and making a bridge to cross the river, he came speedily by a little-known path to the city of Nole, where he told Tullydub, the lord high counselor, what was threatening his king.

So, trembling with terror, Tullydub hastened to the palace and called a meeting of the five high counselors in the king's antechamber.

When all were assembled, together with Bud and Fluff, the old man told his news and cried:

"We shall all be slaughtered and our kingdom sacked and destroyed, for the army of Ix is twice as big as our own—yes, twice as big!"

"Oh, pooh! What of that?" said Tollydob, scornfully; "have they a general as tall as I am?"

"Certainly not," said the chief counselor. "Who ever saw a man as tall as you are?"

"Then I'll fight and conquer them!" declared Tollydob, rising and walking about the room, so that all might see where his head just grazed the ceiling.

"But you can't, general; you can't fight an army by yourself!" remonstrated Tullydub, excitedly. "And being so big, you are a better mark for their arrows and axes."

At this the general sat down rather suddenly and grew pale.

"Perhaps we can buy them off," remarked the lord

high purse-bearer, jingling the purse that now never became empty.

"No, I 'm afraid not," sighed Tullydub. "Quavo the minstrel said they were bent upon conquest, and were resolved upon a battle."

The general sat down suddenly and grew pale.

"And their queen is a witch," added Tallydab, nervously. "We must not forget that."

"A witch!" exclaimed Princess Fluff, with sudden interest. "What does she look like?"

But all shook their heads at the question, and Tullydub explained:

"None of us has ever seen her, for we have never been friendly with the people of Ix. But from all reports, Queen Zixi is both young and beautiful."

"Maybe it 's the one who wanted to teach me witchcraft in order to steal my magic cloak!" said Fluff, with sudden excitement. "And when she found she could n't steal it, she went back after her army."

"What magic cloak do you refer to?" asked Tullydub.

"Why, the one the fairies gave me," replied Fluff.

"Is it of gorgeous colors with golden threads running through it?" asked the lord high general, now thoroughly interested.

"Yes," said the princess, "the very same."

"And what peculiar powers does it possess?"

"Why, it grants its wearer the fulfilment of one wish," she answered.

All the high counselors regarded her earnestly.

"Then that was the cloak I wore when I wished to be ten feet high!" said Tollydob.

"And I wore it when I wished I could reach the apple," said Tellydeb.

"And I wore it when I wished that my dog Ruffles could speak," said Tallydab.

"And I wore it when I wished the royal purse would always remain full," said Tillydib.

"I did not know that," remarked Fluff, thoughtfully. "But I 'll never forget that I lent it to Aunt Rivette, and that was the time she wished she could fly!"

"Why, it 's wonderful!" cried old Tullydub. "Has it granted you, also, a wish?"

"Yes," said Fluff, brightly. "And I 've been happy ever since."

"And has your brother, the king, had a wish?" Tullydub inquired eagerly.

"No," said Bud. "I can still have mine."

"Then why does n't your Majesty wear the cloak and wish that your army shall conquer the Queen of Ix's?" asked the lord high counselor.

"I 'm saving my wish," answered Bud, "and it won't be that, either."

"But unless something is done we shall all be destroyed," protested Tullydub.

"Then wear the cloak yourself," said Bud. "You have n't had a wish yet."

"Good!" cried the four other counselors; and the lord high general added:

"That will surely save us from any further worry."

"I 'll fetch the cloak at once," said Fluff, and she ran quickly from the room to get it.

"Supposing," Tullydub remarked hesitatingly, "the magic power should n't work?"

"Oh, but it will!" answered the general.

"I 'm sure it will," said the steward.

"I know it will," declared the purse-bearer.

"It cannot fail," affirmed the executioner; "remember what it has already done for us!"

Then Fluff arrived with the cloak; and, after considering carefully how he would speak his wish, the lord high counselor drew the cloak over his shoulders and said solemnly:

"I wish that we shall be

The counselor drew the cloak over his shoulders.

able to defeat our enemies, and drive them all from the kingdom of Noland."

"Did n't you make two wishes instead of one?" asked the princess, anxiously.

"Never mind," said the general; "if we defeat them it will be easy enough to drive them from our kingdom."

The lord high counselor removed the cloak and carefully refolded it.

"If it grants my wish," said he, thoughtfully, "it

will indeed be lucky for our country that the Princess
Fluff came to live in the palace of the king."

The queen formed her men into a line of battle
facing the army of Nole, and they were so numerous
in comparison with their enemies that even the more
timorous soldiers gained confidence, and stood up
straight and threw out their chests as if to show how
brave they were.

Then Queen Zixi, clad in her flashing mail and
mounted upon her magnificent white charger, rode
slowly along the ranks, her white plume nodding
gracefully with the motion of the horse.

And when she reached the center of the line she
halted, and addressed her army in a voice that sounded
clear as the tones of a bell and reached to every listening ear.

"Soldiers of the land of Ix," she began, "we are
about to engage in a great battle for conquest and
glory. Before you lies the rich city of Nole, and
when you have defeated yonder army and gained the
gates you may divide among yourselves all the plun-
der of gold and silver and jewels and precious stones
that the place contains."

Hearing this, a great shout of joy arose from the
soldiers, which Zixi quickly silenced with a wave of
her white hand.

"For myself," she continued, "I desire nothing

more than a cloak that is owned by the Princess Fluff. All else shall be given to my brave army."

"But—suppose we do not win the battle?" asked one of her generals, anxiously. "What then do we gain?"

"Nothing but disgrace," answered the queen, haughtily. "But how can we fail to win when I myself lead the assault? Queen Zixi of Ix has fought

The lord high executioner suddenly stretched out his long arm, and

a hundred battles and never yet met with defeat!"

There was more cheering at this, for Zixi's words were quite true. Nevertheless, her soldiers did not like the look of that silent army of Nole standing so steadfastly before the gates and facing the invaders with calm determination.

Zixi herself was somewhat disturbed at this sight, for she could not guess what powers the magic cloak had given to the Nolanders. But in a loud and un-daunted voice she shouted the command to advance; and while trumpets blared and drums rolled, the great army of Ix awoke to action and marched steadily upon the men of Nole.

Bud, who could not bear to remain shut up in his palace while all this excitement was occurring outside the city gates, had slipped away from Fluff and joined his gigantic general, Tollydob. He was, of course, unused to war, and when he beheld the vast array of Zixi's army he grew fearful that the magic cloak might not be able to save his city from conquest.

reached the far-away general of Ix, and pulled him from his horse.

Yet the five high counselors, who were all present, seemed not to worry the least bit.

"They 're very pretty soldiers to look at," remarked old Tollydob, complacently. "I 'm really sorry to defeat them, they march so beautifully."

"But do not let your kind-hearted admiration for the enemy interfere with our plans," said the lord high executioner, who was standing by with his hands in his pockets.

"Oh, I won't!" answered the big general, with a laugh which was succeeded by a frown. "Yet I can never resist admiring a fine soldier, whether he fights for or against me. For instance, just look at that handsome officer riding beside Queen Zixi—her chief general, I think. Is n't he sweet? He looks just like an apple, he is so round and wears such a tight-fitting red jacket. Can't you pick him for me, friend Tellydeb?"

"I 'll try." And the lord high executioner suddenly stretched out his long arm, and reached the far-away general of Ix, and pulled him from the back of his horse.

Then, amid the terrified cries that came from the opposing army, Tellydeb dragged his victim swiftly over the ground until he was seized by the men of Nole and firmly bound with cords.

"Thank you, my friend," said the general, again laughing and then frowning. "Now get for me that pretty queen, if you please."

Once more the long arm of the lord high executioner shot out toward the army of Ix. But Zixi's keen eyes saw it coming, and instantly she disappeared, her magical arts giving her power to become invisible.

Tellydeb, puzzled to find the queen gone, seized another officer instead of her and dragged him quickly over the intervening space to his own side, where he was bound by the Nolanders and placed beside his fellow-captive.

Another cry of horror came from the army of Ix, and with one accord the soldiers stopped short in their advance. Queen Zixi, appearing again in their midst, called upon her wavering soldiers to charge quickly upon the foe.

But the men, bewildered and terrified, were deaf to her appeals. They fled swiftly back, over the brow of the hill, and concealed themselves in the wooded valley until the sun set. And it was far into the night before Queen Zixi succeeded in restoring her line of battle.

Chapter XIV.

THE ROUT OF THE ARMY OF IX.

The next day was a busy one in the city of Nole. The ten-foot lord high general marched his seven thousand seven hundred and seventy-seven men out of the city gates and formed them in line of battle on the brow of a hill. Then he asked Aunt Rivette to fly over the top of the mountain and see where the enemy was located.

The old woman gladly undertook the mission. She had by this time become an expert flier, and, being proud to resemble a bird, she dressed herself in flowing robes of as many colors as a poll-parrot could boast. When she mounted into the air, streamers of green and yellow silk floated behind her in quite a beautiful and interesting fashion, and she was admired by all beholders.

Aunt Rivette flew high above the mountain-top, and there she saw the great army of Queen Zixi climbing up the slope on the other side. The army also saw her, and stopped short in amazement at seeing a woman fly like a bird. They had before this thought their queen sure of victory, because she was a witch and possessed many wonderful arts; but now they saw that the people of Noland could also do wonderful things, and it speedily disheartened them.

Zixi ordered them to shoot a thousand arrows at Aunt Rivette, but quickly countermanded the order, as the old woman was too high to be injured, and the arrows would have been wasted.

When the army of Ix had climbed the mountain and was marching down again toward Nole, the lord

F. RICHARDSON

And Ruffles would pretend to be scratching his nose.

high steward sent his dog Ruffles to them to make more mischief. Ruffles trotted soberly among the soldiers of Ix, and once in a while he would pause and say in a loud voice:

"The army of Noland will conquer you."

Then all the soldiers would look around to see who had spoken these fearful words, but could see nothing but a little dog; and Ruffles would pretend to be scratching his nose with his left hind foot, and would look so innocent that they never for a moment suspected he could speak.

"We are surrounded by invisible foes!" cried the soldiers; and they would have fled even then had not

The gigantic ten-foot general of the army of Nole stepped in front of his men.

Queen Zixi called them cowards and stubbornly declared that they only fancied they had heard the voices speak. Some of them believed her, and some did not; but they decided to remain and fight, since they had come so far to do so.

Then they formed in line of battle again and marched boldly toward the army of Noland.

While they were still a good way off, and the generals were riding in front of their soldiers, the lord high executioner suddenly stretched out his long arm and pulled another general of Ix from his horse, as he had done the day before, dragging him swiftly over the ground between the opposing armies until he was seized by the men of Nole and tightly bound with cords.

The soldiers of Ix uttered murmurs of horror at this sight, and stopped again.

Immediately the long arm shot out, and pulled another general from their ranks, and made him prisoner.

Queen Zixi raved and stormed with anger; but the lord high executioner, who was enjoying himself immensely, continued to grab officer after officer and make them prisoners: and so far there had been no sign of battle; not an arrow had been fired nor an ax swung.

Then, to complete the amazement of the enemy, the gigantic ten-foot general of the army of Nole stepped in front of his men and waved around his head a flashing sword six feet in length, while he shouted in a voice like a roar of thunder, that made the army of Ix tremble:

"Forward, soldiers of Noland—forward! Destroy the enemy, and let none escape!"

It was more than the army of Ix could bear. Filled with terror, the soldiers threw down their arms and fled in a great panic, racing over the mountain-top and down the other side and then scattering in every direction, each man for himself and as if he feared the entire army of Noland was at his heels.

Bud was so amused at the sight of the flying foe that he rolled on the ground in laughter.

But it was n't. Not a soldier of Nole had moved in pursuit. Every one was delighted at the easy victory, and King Bud was so amused at the sight of the flying foe that he rolled on the ground in laughter, and even the fierce-looking General Tollydob grinned in sympathy.

Then, with bands playing and banners flying, the entire army marched back into the city, and the war between Noland and Ix was over.

Chapter XV.

THE THEFT OF THE MAGIC CLOAK.

WHEN the soldiers of Queen Zixi ran away, they fled in so many different directions that the bewildered queen could not keep track of them. Her horse, taking fright, dashed up the mountain-side and tossed Zixi into a lilac-bush, after which he ran off and left her.

One would think such a chain of misfortunes could not fail to daunt the bravest. But Zixi had lived too many years to allow such trifles as defeat and flight to ruin her nerves; so she calmly disentangled herself from the lilac-bush and looked around to see where she was.

It was very quiet and peaceful on this part of the mountain-side. Her glittering army had disappeared to the last man.

In the far distance she could see the spires and turreted palaces of the city of Nole, and behind her was a thick grove of lilac-trees bearing flowers in full bloom.

This lilac-grove gave Zixi an idea. She pushed aside some of the branches and entered the cool, shadowy avenues between the trees.

The air was heavy with the scent of the violet flowers, and tiny humming-birds were darting here and there to thrust their long bills into the blossoms and draw out the honey for food. Butterflies there were, too, and a few chipmunks perched high among the branches. But Zixi walked on through the trees in deep thought, and presently she had laid new plans.

For since the magic cloak was so hard to get she wanted it more than ever.

By and by she gathered some bits of the lilac-bark, and dug some roots from the ground. Next she caught six spotted butterflies, from the wings of which she brushed off all the round, purple spots. Then she wandered on until she came upon a little spring of water bubbling from the ground, and filling a cup-shaped leaf of the tatti-plant from the spring, she mixed her bark and roots and butterfly-spots in the liquid and boiled it carefully over a fire of twigs; for tatti-leaves will not burn so long as there is water inside them.

When her magical compound was ready, Zixi muttered an incantation and drank it in a single draught.

A few moments later the witch-queen had disappeared, and in her place stood the likeness of a pretty young girl dressed in a simple white gown with pink ribbons at the shoulders and a pink sash around her waist. Her light-brown hair was gathered into two long braids that hung down her back, and she had two big blue eyes that looked very innocent and sweet.

Besides these changes, both the nose and the mouth of the girl differed in shape from those of Zixi, so that no one would have seen the slightest resemblance between the two people, or between Miss Trust and the girl who stood in the lilac-grove.

The transformed witch-queen gave a sweet, rippling laugh, and glanced at her reflection in the still waters of the spring. And then the girlish face frowned, for the image glaring up at her was that of a wrinkled, toothless old hag.

"I really must have that cloak," sighed the girl; and then she turned and walked out of the lilac-grove and down the mountain-side toward the city of Nole.

The Princess Fluff was playing tennis with her maids in a courtyard of the royal palace, when Jikki came to say that a girl wished to speak with her Highness.

"Send her here," said Fluff.

So the witch-queen came to her, in the guise of the fair young girl; and bowing in a humble manner before the princess, she said: "Please, your Highness, may I be one of your maids?"

"Why, I have eight already!" answered Fluff, laughing.

"But my father and mother are both dead; and I have come all the way from my castle to beg you to let me wait upon you," said the girl, looking at the little princess with a pleading expression in her blue eyes.

"Who are you?" asked Fluff.

"I am daughter of the Lord Hurrydole, and my name is Adlena," replied the girl, which was not altogether a falsehood, because one of her ancestors had borne the name Hurrydole, and Adlena was one of her own names.

"Then, Adlena," said Fluff, brightly, "you shall certainly be one of my maids; for there is plenty of room in the palace, and the more girls I have around me the happier I shall be."

So Queen Zixi, under the name of Adlena, became an inmate of the king's palace; and it was not many days before she learned where the magic cloak was kept. For the princess gave her a key to a drawer and told her to get from it a blue silk scarf she wished to wear, and directly under the scarf lay the fairy garment.

Adlena would have seized it at that moment had she dared; but Fluff was in the same room, so she only said: "Please, princess, may I look at that pretty cloak?"

"Of course," answered Fluff; "but handle it carefully, for it was given me by the fairies."

So Adlena unfolded the cloak and looked at it very carefully, noting exactly the manner in which it was woven. Then she folded it again, arranged it in the drawer, and turned the key, which the princess immediately attached to a chain which she always wore around her neck.

That night, when the witch-queen was safely locked

in her own room and could not be disturbed, she called about her a great many of those invisible imps that serve the most skilful witches, commanding them to weave for her a cloak in the exact likeness of the one given Princess Fluff by the fairies.

Of course the imps had never seen the magic cloak; but Zixi described it to them accurately, and before morning they had woven a garment so closely resembling the original that the imitation was likely to deceive any one.

Only one thing was missing, and that was the golden thread woven by Queen Lulea herself, and which gave the cloak its magic powers.

Of course the imps of Zixi could not get this golden thread, nor could they give any magical properties to the garment they had made at the witch's command; but they managed to give the cloak all of the many brilliant colors of the original, and Zixi was quite satisfied.

The next day Adlena wore this cloak while she walked in the garden. Very soon Princess Fluff saw her and ran after the girl, crying indignantly: "See here! What do you mean by wearing my cloak? Take it off instantly!"

"It is n't your cloak. It is one of my own," replied the girl, calmly.

"Nonsense! There can't be two such cloaks in the world," retorted Fluff.

"But there are," persisted Adlena. "How could

I get the one in your drawer when the key is around
your own neck?"

"I 'm sure I don't know," admitted the princess,
beginning to be puzzled. "But come with me into
my rooms. If my fairy cloak is indeed in the drawer,
then I will believe you."

So they went to the drawer, and of course found
the magic cloak, as the cunning Zixi had planned.
Fluff pulled it out and held the two up together to
compare them; and they seemed to be exactly alike.

"I think yours is a little the longer," said Adlena,
and threw it over the shoulders of the princess. "No,
I think mine is the longer," she continued; and re-
moving the magic cloak, put her own upon Fluff.
They seemed to be about the same length, but Adlena
kept putting first one and then the other upon the
princess, until they were completely mixed, and the
child could not have told one from the other.

"Which is mine?" she finally asked, in a startled
voice.

"This, of course," answered Adlena, folding up the
imitation cloak which the imps had made, and putting
it away in the drawer.

Fluff never suspected the trick, so Zixi carried away
the magic cloak she had thus cleverly stolen; and
she was so delighted with the success of her stratagem
that she could have screamed aloud for pure joy.

As soon as she was alone and unobserved, the
witch-queen slipped out of the palace, and, carrying

the magic cloak in a bundle under her arm, ran down the streets of Nole and out through the gate in the wall and away toward the mountain where the lilac-grove lay.

"Which is mine?" she finally asked, in a startled voice.

"At last!" she kept saying to herself. "At last I shall see my own beautiful reflection in a mirror, instead of that horrid old hag!"

When she was safe in the grove she succeeded, by means of her witchcraft, in transforming the girl Adlena back into the beautiful woman known throughout the kingdom of Ix as Queen Zixi. And then she lost no time in throwing the magic cloak over her shoulders.

"I wish," she cried in a loud voice, "that my reflection in every mirror will hereafter show the same face and form as that in which I appear to exist in the sight of all mortals!"

Then she threw off the cloak and ran to the crystal spring, saying: "Now, indeed, I shall at last see the lovely Queen Zixi!"

But as she bent over the spring, she gave a sudden shriek of disappointed rage; for glaring up at her from the glassy surface of the water was the same fearful hag she had always seen as the reflection of her likeness!

The magic cloak would grant no wish to a person who had stolen it.

Zixi, more wretched than she had ever been before in her life, threw herself down upon her face in the lilac-grove and wept for more than an hour, which is an exceedingly long time for tears to run from one's eyes. And when she finally arose, two tiny brooks flowed from the spot and wound through the lilac-trees—one to the right and one to the left.

Then, leaving the magic cloak—to possess which she had struggled so hard and sinfully—lying unheeded upon the ground, the disappointed witch-queen walked slowly away, and finally reached the bank of the great river.

Here she found a rugged old alligator who lay upon the bank, weeping with such bitterness that the sight reminded Zixi of her own recent outburst of

She threw off the cloak and ran to the crystal spring.

sorrow.

"Why do you weep, friend?" she asked, for her experience as a witch had long since taught her the language of the beasts and birds and reptiles.

"Because I cannot climb a tree," answered the alligator.

"Because I cannot climb a tree," answered the alligator.

"But why do you wish to climb a tree?" she questioned, surprised.

"Because I can't," returned the alligator, squeezing two more tears from his eyes.

"But that is very foolish!" exclaimed the witch-queen, scornfully.

"Oh, I don't know," said the alligator. "It does n't strike me that it 's much more foolish than the fancies some other people have."

"Why do you wail so loudly?" she asked.

"Perhaps not," replied Zixi, more gently, and walked away in deep thought.

While she followed the river-bank, to find a ferry across, the dusk fell, and presently a gray owl came out of a hollow in a tall tree and sat upon a limb, wailing dismally.

Zixi stopped and looked at the bird.

"Why do you wail so loudly?" she asked.

"Because I cannot swim in the river like a fish," answered the owl, and it screeched so sadly that it made the queen shiver.

"Why do you wish to swim?" she inquired.

"Because I can't," said the owl, and buried its head under its wing with a groan.

"But that is absurd!" cried Zixi, with impatience.

The owl had an ear out, and heard her. So it withdrew its head long enough to retort:

"I don't think it's any more absurd than the longings of some other folks."

"Perhaps you are right," said the queen, and hung her head as she walked on.

By and by she found a ferryman with a boat, and he agreed to row her across the river. In one end of the boat crouched a little girl, the ferryman's daughter, and she sobbed continually, so that the sound of the child's grief finally attracted Zixi's attention.

"Why do you sob?" questioned the queen.

"Because I want to be a man," replied the child, trying to stifle her sobs.

"Why do you want to be a man?" asked Zixi, curiously.

"Because I'm a little girl," was the reply.

This made Zixi angry.

"You're a little fool!" she exclaimed loudly.

"There are other fools in the world," said the child, and renewed her sobs.

Zixi did not reply, but she thought to herself:
"We are all alike — the alligator, the owl, the girl,

"Why do you sob?" questioned the queen.

and the powerful Queen of Ix.   We long for what
we cannot have, yet desire it not so much because it
would benefit us, as because it is beyond our reach.
If I call the others fools, I must also call myself a
fool for wishing to see the reflection of a beautiful
girl in my mirror when I know it is impossible.   So
hereafter I shall strive to be contented with my lot."

This was a wise resolution, and the witch-queen
abided by it for many years.   She was not very bad,
this Zixi; for it must be admitted that few have the
courage to acknowledge their faults and strive to cor-
rect them, as she did.

Chapter XVI.

THE PLAIN ABOVE THE CLOUDS.

I have already mentioned how high the mountains were between Noland and the land of Ix; but at the north of the city of Nole were mountains much higher —so high, indeed, that they seemed to pierce the clouds, and it was said the moon often stopped on the highest peak to rest. It was not one single slope up from the lowlands; but first there was a high mountain, with a level plain at the top; and then another high mountain, rising from the level and capped with a second plain; and then another mountain, and so on; which made them somewhat resemble a pair of stairs. So that the people of Nole, who looked upon the North Mountains with much pride, used to point them out as "The Giant's Stairway," forgetting that no giant was ever big enough to use such an immense flight of stairs.

Many people had climbed the first mountain, and upon the plain at its top flocks of sheep were fed; and two or three people boasted they had climbed the second steep; but beyond that the mountains were all unknown to the dwellers in the valley of Noland. As a matter of fact, no one lived upon

them; they were inhabited only by a few small ani-
mals and an occasional vulture or eagle which nested
in some rugged crag.

But at the top of all was an enormous plain that
lay far above the clouds, and here the Roly-Rogues
dwelt in great numbers.

I must describe these Roly-Rogues to you, for they
were unlike any other people in all the world. Their
bodies were as round as a ball—if you can imagine
a ball fully four feet in thickness at the middle. And
their muscles were as tough and elastic as india-rub-
ber. They had heads and arms resembling our own,
and very short legs; and all these they could withdraw into their ball-like bodies whenever they wished,
very much as a turtle withdraws its legs and head
into its shell.

The Roly-Rogues lived all by themselves in their
country among the clouds, and there were thousands
and thousands of them. They were quarrelsome by
nature, but could seldom hurt one another; because,
if they fought, they would withdraw their arms and
legs and heads into their bodies, and roll themselves
at one another with much fierceness. But when they
collided they would bounce apart again, and little
harm was done.

In spite of their savage dispositions the Roly-
Rogues had as yet done no harm to any one but
themselves, as they lived so high above the world
that other people knew nothing of their existence.

All the hundreds and thousands of Roly-Rogues that were in existence assembled upon the edge of their plain, and, at the

F RICHARSON

word of their ruler, hurled
themselves down the mountain
with terrible cries and went
bounding away toward the
peaceful city of Nole.

Nor did they themselves know, because of the clouds that floated between, of the valleys which lay below them.

But, as ill luck would have it, a few days after King Bud's army had defeated the army of Ix, one of the Roly-Rogues, while fighting with another, rolled too near the edge of the plain whereon they dwelt, and bounded down the mountain-side that faced Noland. Wind had scattered the clouds, so his fellows immediately rolled themselves to the edge and watched the luckless Roly-Rogue fly down the mountain, bounce across the plain, and thence speed down the next mountain. By and by he became a dot to their eyes, and then a mere speck; but as the clouds had just rolled away for a few moments the Roly-Rogues could see, by straining their eyes, the city of Nole lying in the valley far below.

It seemed, from that distance, merely a toy city, but they knew it must be a big place to show so far away; and since they had no cities of their own, they became curious to visit the one they had just discovered.

The ruler of the Roly-Rogues, who was more quarrelsome than any of the rest, had a talk with his chief men about visiting the unknown city.

"We can roll down the mountain just as our brother did," he argued.

"But how in the world could we ever get back again?" said one of the chiefs, sticking his head up to look with astonishment at the ruler.

"We don't want to get back," said the other, excitedly. "Some one has built many houses and palaces at the foot of the mountains, and we can live in those, if they are big enough and if there are enough of them."

"Perhaps the people won't let us," suggested another chief, who was not in favor of the expedition.

"We will fight them and destroy them," retorted the ruler, scowling at the chief as if he would make him ashamed of his cowardice.

"Then we must all go together," said a third chief; "for, if only a few go, we may find ourselves many times outnumbered and at last be overcome."

"Every Roly-Rogue in the country shall go!" declared the ruler, who brooked no opposition when once he had made up his mind to a thing.

On the plain grew a grove of big thorn-trees, bearing thorns as long and sharp as swords; so the ruler commanded each of his people to cut two of the thorns, one for each hand, with which to attack whatever foes they might meet when they reached the unknown valley.

Then, on a certain day, all the hundreds and thousands of Roly-Rogues that were in existence assembled upon the edge of their plain, and, at the word of their ruler, hurled themselves down the mountain with terrible cries and went bounding away toward the peaceful city of Nole.

Chapter XVII.

THE DESCENT OF THE ROLY-ROGUES.

KING BUD and Princess Fluff were leading very happy and peaceful lives in their beautiful palace. All wars and dangers seemed at an end, and there was nothing to disturb their content.

All the gold that was needed the royal purse-bearer was able to supply from his overflowing purse. The gigantic General Tollydob became famous throughout the world, and no nation dared attack the army of Noland. The talking dog of old Tallydab made every one wonder, and people came many miles to see Ruffles and hear him speak. It was said that all this good fortune had been brought to Noland by the pretty Princess Fluff, who was a favorite of the fairies; and the people loved her on this account as well as for her bright and sunny disposition.

King Bud caused his subjects some little anxiety, to be sure; for they never could tell what he was liable to do next, except that he was sure to do something unexpected. But much is forgiven a king; and if Bud made some pompous old nobleman stand on his head, to amuse a mob of people, he would give him a good dinner afterward and fill his purse with

gold to make up for the indignity.   Fluff often re-
proved her brother for such pranks, but Bud's soul
was flooded with mischief, and it was hard for him
to resist letting a little of the surplus escape now and
then.

The great ball struck the field near them.

After all, the people were fairly content and pros-
perous, and no one was at all prepared for the disas-
ters soon to overtake them.

One day, while King Bud was playing at ball with
some of his courtiers on a field outside the city gates,

the first warning of trouble reached him.   Bud had batted a ball high into the air, and while looking upward for it to descend he saw another ball bound from the plain at the top of the North Mountains, fly into the air, and then sink gradually toward him. As it approached, it grew bigger and bigger, until it assumed mammoth proportions; and then, while the courtiers screamed in terror, the great ball struck the field near them, bounced high into the air, and came down directly upon the sharp point of one of the palace towers, where it stuck fast with a yell that sounded almost human.

For some moments Bud and his companions were motionless through surprise and fear; then they rushed into the city and stood among the crowd of people which had congregated at the foot of the tower to stare at the big ball impaled upon its point.   Once in a while, two arms, two short legs, and a head would dart out from the ball and wiggle frantically, and then the yell would be repeated and the head and limbs withdrawn swiftly into the ball.

It was all so curious that the people were justified in staring at it in amazement; for certainly no one had ever seen or heard of a Roly-Rogue before, or even known such a creature existed.

Finally, as no one else could reach the steeple-top, Aunt Rivette flew into the air and circled slowly around the ball.   When next its head was thrust out, she called:

"Where did you come from?" asked Aunt Rivette.

"Are you a mud-turtle or a man?"

"I 'll show you which, if I get hold of you," answered the Roly-Rogue, fiercely.

"Where did you come from?" asked Aunt Rivette, taking care the wiggling arms did not grab her.

"That is none of your business," said the Roly-Rogue. "But I did n't intend to come, that you may depend upon."

"Are you hurt?" she inquired, seeing that the struggles of the creature made him spin around upon the steeple-point like a windmill.

"No, I 'm not hurt at all," declared the Roly-Rogue; "but I 'd like to know how to get down."

"What would you do if we helped you to get free?" asked Aunt Rivette.

"I 'd fight every one of those idiots who are laughing at me down there!" said the creature, its eyes flashing wickedly.

"Then you 'd best stay where you are," returned old Rivette, who flew back to earth again to tell Bud what the Roly-Rogue had said.

"I believe that is the best place for him," said Bud; "so we 'll let him stay where he is. He 's not very ornamental, I must say, but he 's very safe up there on top of the steeple."

"We might have him gilded," proposed the old woman, "and then he 'd look better."

"I 'll think it over," said the king, and he went away to finish his ball game.

The people talked and wondered about the queer creature on the steeple, but no one could say where it came from or what it was; they were naturally much puzzled.

The next day was bright with sunshine; so, early in the forenoon, Bud and Fluff had the royal cook fill their baskets with good things to eat, and set out to picnic on the bank of the river that separated No-land from the kingdom of Ix. They rode ponies, to reach the river sooner than by walking; and their only companions were Tallydab, the lord high steward, and his talking dog, Ruffles.

It was after this picnic party had passed over the mountain, and were securely hidden from any one in the city of Nole, that the ruler of the Roly-Rogues and his thousands of followers hurled themselves down from their land above the clouds and began bounding toward the plain below.

The people first heard a roar that sounded like distant thunder; and when they looked toward the North Mountains they saw the air black with tiny bouncing balls that seemed to drop from the drifting clouds which always had obscured the highest peak.

But, although appearing small when first seen, these balls grew rapidly larger as they came nearer; and then, with sharp reports like pistol-shots, they began dropping upon the plain by dozens and hundreds and then thousands.

As soon as they touched the ground they bounded

upward again, like rubber balls the children throw upon the floor; but each bound was less violent than the one preceding it, until finally within the streets of the city and upon all the fields surrounding it lay the thousands of Roly-Rogues that had fallen from the mountain-peak.

At first they lay still, as if stunned by their swift journey and collision with the hard earth; but after a few seconds they recovered, thrust out their heads and limbs, and scrambled upon their flat feet.

Then the savage Roly-Rogues uttered hoarse shouts of joy, for they were safely arrived at the city they had seen from afar, and the audacious adventure was a success.

Chapter XVIII.

THE CONQUEST OF NOLAND.

It would be impossible to describe the amazement of the people of Nole when the Roly-Rogues came upon them.

Not only was the descent wholly unexpected, but the appearance of the invaders was queer enough to strike terror to the stoutest heart.

Their round bodies were supported by short, strong legs having broad, flattened feet to keep them steady. Their arms were short, and the fingers of their hands, while not long, were very powerful.

But the heads were the most startling portions of these strange creatures. They were flat and thick on the top, with leathery rolls around their necks; so that, when the head was drawn in, its upper part rounded out the surface of the ball. In this peculiar head the Roly-Rogue had two big eyes as shiny as porcelain, a small stubby nose, and a huge mouth. Their strange leather-like clothing fitted their bodies closely and was of different colors—green, yellow, red, and brown.

Taken altogether, the Roly-Rogues were not pretty to look at; and although their big eyes gave them a startled or astonished expression, nothing seemed ever to startle or astonish them in the least.

When they arrived in the valley of Nole, after their wonderful journey down the mountains, they scrambled to their feet, extended their long arms with the

As for the women and children,

thorns clasped tight in their talon-like fingers, and rushed in a furious crowd and with loud cries upon the terror-stricken people.

The soldiers of Tollydob's brave army had not even time to seize their weapons; for such a foe, coming upon them through the air, had never been dreamed of.

And the men of Nole, who might have resisted

the enemy, were too much frightened to do more than
tremble violently and gasp with open mouths.   As
for the women and children, they fled screaming into
the houses and bolted or locked the doors, which was

they fled screaming into the houses.

doubtless the wisest thing they could have done.

General Tollydob was asleep when the calamity of
this invasion occurred; but hearing the shouts, he ran
out of his mansion and met several of the Roly-Rogues
face to face.   Without hesitation the brave general
rushed upon them; but two of the creatures promptly
rolled themselves against him from opposite directions, so that the ten-foot giant was crushed between

them until there was not a particle of breath left in his body. No sooner did these release him than two other Roly-Rogues rolled toward him; but Tollydob was not to be caught twice, so he gave a mighty jump and jumped right over their heads, with the result that the balls crashed against each other.

This made the two Roly-Rogues so angry that they began to fight each other savagely, and the general started to run away. But other foes rolled after him, knocked him down, and stuck their thorns into him until he yelled for mercy and promised to become their slave.

Tullydub, the chief counselor, watched all this from his window, and it frightened him so greatly that he crawled under his bed and hid, hoping the creatures would not find him. But their big round eyes were sharp at discovering things; so the Roly-Rogues had not been in Tullydub's room two minutes before he was dragged from beneath his bed, and prodded with thorns until he promised obedience to the conquerors.

The lord high purse-bearer, at the first alarm, dug a hole in the garden of the royal palace and buried his purse so no one could find it but himself. But he might have saved himself this trouble, for the Roly-Rogues knew nothing of money or its uses, being accustomed to seizing whatever they desired without a thought of rendering payment for it.

Having buried his purse, old Tillydib gave himself up to the invaders as their prisoner; and this saved him the indignity of being conquered.

The lord high executioner may really be credited with making the only serious fight of the day; for when the Roly-Rogues came upon him, Tellydeb

Other foes rolled after him and knocked him down.

seized his ax, and, before the enemy could come near, he reached out his long arm and cleverly sliced the heads off several of their round bodies.

The others paused for a moment, being unused to such warfare and not understanding how an arm could reach so far.

But, seeing their heads were in danger, about a hundred of the creatures formed themselves into balls and rolled upon the executioner in a straight line, hoping to crush him.

Stepping aside, Tellydeb aimed a strong blow with his ax at the body of the first Roly-Rogue.

They could not see what happened after they began to roll, their heads being withdrawn; but Tellydeb watched them speed toward him, and, stepping aside, he aimed a strong blow with his ax at the body of the first Roly-Rogue that passed him. Instead of cutting the rubber-like body, the ax bounced back and flew from Tellydeb's hand into the air, falling farther away than the long arm of the executioner could reach. Therefore he was left helpless, and was wise enough to surrender without further resistance.

Finding no one else to resist them, the Roly Rogues contented themselves with bounding against the terrorized people, great and humble alike, and knocking them over, laughing boisterously at the fig-ures sprawling in the mud of the streets.

And then they would prick the bodies of the men with their sharp thorns, making them spring to their feet again with shrieks of fear, only to be bowled over again the next minute.

But the monsters soon grew weary of this amuse-ment, for they were anxious to explore the city they had so successfully invaded. They flocked into the palace and public buildings, and gazed eagerly at the many beautiful and, to them, novel things that were found. The mirrors delighted them, and they fought one another for the privilege of standing before the glasses to admire the reflection of their horrid bodies.

They could not sit in the chairs, for the round bodies would not fit them; neither could the Roly-Rogues understand the use of beds. For when they rested or slept the creatures merely withdrew their limbs and heads, rolled over upon their backs, and slept soundly—no matter where they might be.

The shops were all entered and robbed of their wares, the Roly-Rogues wantonly destroying all that they could not use. They were like ostriches in eat-ing anything that looked attractive to them; one of the monsters swallowed several pretty glass beads, and some of the more inquisitive of them invaded the grocery-shops and satisfied their curiosity by tasting of nearly everything in sight.   It was funny to see their wry faces when they sampled the salt and vinegar.

Presently the entire city was under the dominion of the Roly-Rogues, who forced the unhappy people to wait upon them and amuse them; and if any hesitated to obey their commands, the monsters would bump against them, pull their hair, and make them suffer most miserably.

Aunt Rivette was in her room at the top of the palace when the Roly-Rogues invaded the city of Nole.   At first she was as much frightened as the others; but she soon remembered she could escape the creatures by flying; so she quietly watched them from the windows.   By and by, as they explored the palace, they came to Aunt Rivette's room and broke in the door; but the old woman calmly stepped out of her window upon a little iron balcony, spread her great wings, and flew away before the Roly-Rogues could catch her.

Then she soared calmly through the air, and having remembered that Bud and Fluff had gone to the river on a picnic, she flew swiftly in that direction and before long came to where the children and old Tallydab were eating their luncheon, while the dog Ruffles, who was in good spirits, sang a comic song to amuse them.

They were much surprised to see Aunt Rivette flying toward them; but when she alighted and told Bud that his kingdom had been conquered by the Roly-Rogues and all his people enslaved, the little party was so astonished that they stared at one another in speechless amazement.

"Oh, Bud, what shall we do?" finally asked Fluff, in distress.

"Don't know," said Bud, struggling to swallow a large piece of sandwich that in his excitement had stuck fast in his throat.

"One thing is certain," remarked Aunt Rivette, helping herself to a slice of cake, "our happy lives are now ruined forever. We should be foolish to remain here; and the sooner we escape to some other country where the Roly-Rogues cannot find us, the safer we shall be."

"But why run away?" asked Bud. "Can't something else be done? Here, Tallydab, you're one of my counselors. What do you say about this affair?"

Now the lord high steward was a deliberate old fellow, and before he replied he dusted the crumbs from his lap, filled and lighted his long pipe, and smoked several whiffs in a thoughtful manner.

"It strikes me," said he at last, "that by means of the Princess Fluff's magic cloak we can either destroy or scatter these rascally invaders and restore the kingdom to peace and prosperity."

"Sure enough!" replied Bud. "Why did n't we think of that before?"

"You will have to make the wish, Bud," said Fluff, "for all the rest of us have wished, and you have not made yours yet."

"All right," answered the king. "If I must, I

"But where's the cloak?" asked the dog.

must. But I 'm sorry I have to do it now, for I was saving my wish for something else."

"But where 's the cloak?" asked the dog, rudely breaking into the conversation. "You can't wish without the cloak."

"The cloak is locked up in a drawer in my room at the palace," said Fluff.

"And our enemies have possession of the palace," continued Tallydab, gloomily. "Was there ever such ill luck!"

"Never mind," said Aunt Rivette, "I 'll fly back and get it—that is, if the Roly-Rogues have n't already broken open the drawer and discovered the cloak."

"Please go at once, then!" exclaimed Fluff. "Here is the key," and she unfastened it from the chain at her neck and handed it to her aunt. "But be careful, whatever you do, that those horrible creatures do not catch you."

"I 'm not afraid," said Aunt Rivette, confidently. And taking the key, the old lady at once flew away in the direction of the city of Nole, promising to return very soon.

Chapter XIX.

THE BRAVERY OF AUNT RIVETTE.

The Roly-Rogues were so busy rioting that they did not look into the air and discover Aunt Rivette flying over the city. So she alighted, all unobserved, upon a balcony of the palace, just outside the chamber of the Princess Fluff, and succeeded in entering the room.

The creatures had ransacked this apartment, as they had every other part of the royal palace, and Fluff's pretty dresses and ornaments were strewn about in dreadful confusion. But the drawer in which rested the magic cloak was still locked, and in a few moments the old woman had the precious garment in her hands.

It was, as we know, the imitation cloak Queen Zixi had made and exchanged for the real one; but so closely did it resemble the fairy cloak that Aunt Rivette had no idea she was carrying a useless garment back to her little niece and nephew. On the contrary, she thought to herself: "Now we can quickly dispose of these monstrous rogues and drive them back to their own country."

Hearing some one moving about in the next room, she ran to the window and soon was flying away with the cloak to the place where she had left Bud and Fluff.

"Good!" cried the lord high steward, when he saw the cloak. "Now we have nothing more to fear. Put on your cloak, your Majesty, and make the wish."

Bud threw the cloak over his shoulders.

"What shall I wish?" he asked.

"Let me see," answered Tallydab. "What we want is to get rid of these invaders. Wish them all in the kingdom of Ix."

"Oh, no!" cried Fluff; "it would be wicked to injure Queen Zixi and her people. Let us wish the Roly-Rogues back where they came from."

"That would be folly!" said the dog Ruffles, with an accent of scorn. "For they could easily return again to our city of Nole, having once learned the way there."

"That is true," agreed Aunt Rivette. "The safest thing to do is to wish them all dead."

"But it would be an awful job to bury so many great balls," objected Bud. "It would keep all our people busy for a month, at least."

"Why not wish them dead and buried?" asked Ruffles. "Then they would be out of the way for good and all."

"A capital idea!" responded Tallydab.

"But I have n't seen these curious creatures yet," said Bud; "and if I now wish them all dead and buried, I shall never get a glimpse of one of them.

So let 's walk boldly into the city, and when they
appear to interfere with us I 'll make the wish and
the Roly-Rogues will instantly disappear."

He made old Tullydub, the lord high counselor, rock him
gently as he lay upon his back.

So the entire party returned to the city of Nole;
Bud and Fluff riding their ponies, Aunt Rivette fluttering along beside them, and the lord high steward
walking behind with his dog.

The Roly-Rogues were so much surprised to see
this little party boldly entering the streets of the city,
and showing no particle of fear of them, that they at
first made no offer to molest them.

Even when Bud roared with laughter at their queer
appearance, and called them "mud-turtles" and "foot-

balls," they did not resent the insults; for they had
never heard of either a turtle or a foot-ball before.

When the party had reached the palace and the

Jikki was scratching the back of another Roly-Rogue.

children had dismounted, Bud laughed yet louder;
for the gigantic General Tollydob came to the kitchen
door, wearing an apron while he polished a big
dish-pan, the Roly-Rogues having made him a
scullion.

The ruler of the Roly-Rogues was suffering from
a toothache, so he had rolled himself into a ball and
made old Tullydub, the lord high counselor, rock him
gently as he lay upon his back, just as one would rock
a baby's cradle.

Jikki was scratching the back of another Roly-Rogue with a sharp garden-rake, while Jikki's six servants stood in a solemn row at his back. They would do anything for Jikki, but they would not lift a finger to serve any one else; so the old valet had to do the scratching unaided.

The lord high purse-bearer was waving a fan.

These six young men had proved a great puzzle to the Roly-Rogues, for they found it impossible to touch them or injure them in any way; so, after several vain attempts to conquer them, they decided to leave Jikki's servants alone.

The lord high purse-bearer was waving a fan to keep the flies off two of the slumbering monsters;

and the lord high executioner was feeding another
Roly-Rogue with soup from a great ladle, the creature finding much amusement in being fed in this
manner.

King Bud, feeling sure of making all his enemies
disappear with a wish, found rare sport in watching

*The lord high executioner was feeding another Roly-
Rogue with soup from a great ladle.*

his periwigged counselors thus serving their captors;
so he laughed and made fun of them until the Roly-
Rogue ruler stuck his head out and commanded the
boy to run away.

"Why, you ugly rascal, I'm the King of Noland,"

replied Bud; "so you 'd better show me proper respect."

With that he picked up a good-sized pebble and threw it at the ruler. It struck him just over his aching tooth, and with a roar of anger the Roly-Rogue bounded toward Bud and his party.

The assault was so sudden that they had much ado

The lord high steward and his dog went down before the rush.

to scramble out of the way; and as soon as Bud could escape the rush of the huge ball, he turned squarely around and shouted:

"I wish every one of the Roly-Rogues dead and buried!"

Hearing this and seeing that the king wore the magic cloak, all the high counselors at once raised a joyful shout, and Fluff and Bud gazed upon the Roly-

"I'll soon carry you over the mountain and the river into the kingdom of Ix."

Rogues expectantly, thinking that of course they would disappear.

But Zixi's cloak had no magic powers whatever; and now dozens of the Roly-Rogues, aroused to anger, bounded toward Bud's little party.

I am sure the result would have been terrible had not Aunt Rivette suddenly come to the children's rescue. She threw one lean arm around Bud and the other around Fluff, and then, quickly fluttering her wings, she flew with them to the roof of the palace, which they reached in safety.

The lord high steward and his dog went down before the rush, and the next moment old Tallydab was crying loudly for mercy, while Ruffles limped away to a safe spot beneath a bench under an apple-tree, howling at every step and shouting angry epithets at the Roly-Rogues.

"I wonder what's the matter with the cloak," gasped Bud. "The old thing's a fraud; it did n't work."

"Something went wrong, that 's certain," replied Fluff. "You 're sure you had n't wished before, are n't you?"

"Yes, I 'm sure," said Bud.

"Perhaps," said Aunt Rivette, "the fairies have no power over these horrible creatures."

"That must be it, of course," said the princess. "But what shall we do now? Our country is entirely conquered by these monsters; so it is n't a safe place for us to stay in."

"I believe I can carry you anywhere you'd like to go," said Aunt Rivette. "You're not so very heavy."

"Suppose we go to Queen Zixi, and ask her to protect us?" the princess suggested.

"That's all right, if she does n't bear us a grudge. You know we knocked out her whole army," remarked Bud.

"Quavo the minstrel says she is very beautiful, and kind to her people," said the girl.

"Well, there's no one else we can trust," Bud answered gloomily; "so we may as well try Zixi. But if you drop either of us on the way, Aunt Rivette, I'll have to call in the lord high executioner."

"Never fear," replied the old woman. "If I drop you, you'll never know what has happened. So each one of you put an arm around my neck, and cling tight, and I'll soon carry you over the mountain and the river into the kingdom of Ix."

Chapter XX.

Bud and Fluff were surprised at the magnificence of the city of Ix. The witch-queen had reigned there so many centuries that she found plenty of time to carry out her ideas; and the gardens, shrubbery, and buildings were beautifully planned and cared for.

The splendid palace of the queen was in the center of a delightful park, with white marble walks leading up to the front door.

Aunt Rivette landed the children at the entrance to this royal park, and they walked slowly toward the palace, admiring the gleaming white statues, the fountains and flowers, as they went.

It was beginning to grow dusk, and the lights were gleaming in the palace windows when they reached it. Dozens of liveried servants were standing near the entrance, and some of these escorted the strangers with much courtesy to a reception-room. There a gray-haired master of ceremonies met them and asked in what way he might serve them.

This politeness almost took Bud's breath away, for he had considered Queen Zixi in the light of an enemy rather than a friend; but he decided not to sail under false colors, so he drew himself up in royal fashion, and answered:

"I am King Bud of Noland, and this is my sister, Princess Fluff, and my Aunt Rivette. My kingdom has been conquered by a horde of monsters, and I have come to the Queen of Ix to ask her assistance."

The master of ceremonies bowed low and said:

"I am sure Queen Zixi will be glad to assist your Majesty. Permit me to escort you to rooms, that you may prepare for an interview with her as soon as she can receive you."

So they were led to luxurious chambers, and were supplied with perfumed baths and clean raiment, which proved very refreshing after their tedious journey through the air.

It was now evening; and when they were ushered into the queen's reception-room the palace was brilliantly lighted.

Zixi, since her great disappointment in the lilacgrove, had decided that her longing to behold a beautiful reflection in her mirror was both impossible and foolish; so she had driven the desire from her heart and devoted herself to ruling her kingdom wisely, as she had ruled before the idea of stealing the magic cloak had taken possession of her. And when her mind was in normal condition the witch-queen was very sweet and agreeable in disposition.

So Queen Zixi greeted Bud and his sister and aunt with great kindness, kissing Fluff affectionately upon her cheek and giving her own hand to Bud to kiss.

It is not strange that the children considered her the most beautiful person they had ever beheld; and to them she was as gentle as beautiful, listening with much interest to their tale of the invasion of the Roly-Rogues, and promising to assist them by every means in her power.

This made Bud somewhat ashamed of his past enmity; so he said bluntly: "I am sorry we defeated your army and made them run."

"Why, that was the only thing you could do, when I had invaded your dominion," answered Zixi. "I admit that you were in the right, and that I deserved my defeat."

"But why did you try to conquer us?" asked Fluff.

"Because I wanted to secure the magic cloak, of which I had heard so much," returned the queen, frankly.

"Oh!" said the girl.

"But, of course, you understand that if I had known the magic cloak could not grant any more wishes, I would not have been so eager to secure it," continued Zixi.

"No," said Bud; "the old thing won't work any more; and we nearly got captured by the Roly-Rogues before we found it out."

"Oh, have you the cloak again?" asked Zixi, with a look of astonishment.

"Yes, indeed," returned the princess; "it was locked up in my drawer, and Aunt Rivette managed to get

*Queen Zixi greeted Bud and his sister and aunt with
great kindness.*

it for me before the Roly-Rogues could find it."

"Locked in your drawer?" repeated the witch-queen, musingly. "Then, I am sorry to say, you have not the fairy cloak at all, but the imitation one."

"What do you mean?" asked Fluff, greatly surprised.

"Why, I must make a confession," said Zixi, with a laugh. "I tried many ways to steal your magic cloak. First, I came to Nole as 'Miss Trust.' Do you remember?"

"Oh, yes!" cried Fluff; "and I mistrusted you from the first."

"And then I sent my army to capture the cloak. But, when both of these plans failed, I disguised myself as the girl Adlena."

"Adlena!" exclaimed the princess. "Why, I 've often wondered what became of my maid Adlena, and why she left me so suddenly and mysteriously."

"Well, she exchanged an imitation cloak for the one the fairies had given you," said Zixi, with a smile. "And then she ran away with the precious garment, leaving in your drawer a cloak that resembled the magic garment but had no magical charms."

"How dreadful!" said Fluff.

"But it did me no good," went on the queen, sadly; "for when I made a wish the cloak could not grant it."

"Because it was stolen!" cried the girl, eagerly. "The fairy who gave it to me said that if the cloak was stolen it would never grant a wish to the thief."

"Oh," said Zixi, astonished, "I did not know that."

"Of course not," Fluff replied, with a rather triumphant smile. "But if you had only come to me and told me frankly that you wanted to use the cloak, I would gladly have lent it to you, and then you could have had your wish."

"Because it was stolen!" cried the girl, eagerly.

"Well, well!" said Zixi, much provoked with herself. "To think I have been so wicked all for nothing, when I might have succeeded without the least trouble had I frankly asked for what I wanted!"

"But—see here!" said Bud, beginning to understand the tangle of events; "I must have worn the imitation cloak when I made my wish, and that was the reason that my wish did n't come true."

"To be sure," rejoined Fluff. "And so it is nothing but the imitation cloak we have brought here."

"No wonder it would not destroy and bury the Roly-Rogues!" declared the boy, sulkily. "But if this is the imitation, where, then, is the real magic cloak?"

"Why, I believe I left it in the lilac-grove," replied Zixi.

"Then we must find it at once," said Bud; "for only by its aid can we get rid of those Roly-Rogues."

"And afterward I will gladly lend it to you also; I promise now to lend it to you," said Fluff, turning to the queen; "and your wish will be fulfilled, after all—whatever it may be."

This expression of kindness and good will brought great joy to Zixi, and she seized the generous child in her arms and kissed her with real gratitude.

"We will start for the lilac-grove to-morrow morning," she exclaimed delightedly; "and before night both King Bud and I will have our wishes fulfilled!"

Then the witch-queen led them to her royal banquet-hall, where a most delightful dinner was served. And all the courtiers and officers of Zixi bowed low, first before the King of Noland and then before his sweet little sister, and promised them the friendship of the entire kingdom of Ix.

Quavo the wandering minstrel chanced to be present that evening, and he sang a complimentary song about King Bud; and a wonderful song about the "Flying Lady," meaning Aunt Rivette; and a beautiful song about the lovely Princess Fluff.

So every one was happy and contented, as they all looked forward to the morrow to regain the magic cloak, and by its means to bring an end to all their worries.

Chapter XXI.

THE SEARCH FOR THE MAGIC CLOAK.

The sun had scarcely risen next morning when our friends left the city of Ix in search of the magic cloak. All were mounted on strong horses, with a dozen soldiers riding behind to protect them from harm, while the royal steward of the witch-queen followed with two donkeys laden with hampers of provisions from which to feed the travelers on their way.

It was a long journey to the wide river, but they finally reached it, and engaged the ferryman to take them across. The ferryman did not like to visit the other shore, which was in the kingdom of Noland; for several of the Roly-Rogues had already been seen upon the mountain-top. But the guard of soldiers reassured the man; so he rowed his big boat across with the entire party, and set them safely on the shore. The ferryman's little daughter was in the boat, but she was not sobbing to-day. On the contrary, her face was all smiles.

"Do you not still wish to be a man?" asked Zixi, patting the child's head.

"No, indeed!" answered the little maid. "For I have discovered all men must work very hard to support their wives and children, and to buy them food and raiment. So I have changed my mind about becoming a man, especially as that would be impossible."

It was not far from the ferry to the grove of lilacs, and as they rode along Zixi saw the gray owl sitting contentedly in a tree and pruning its feathers.

"No, indeed," answered the gray owl. "I believe I am safer in a tree."

"Are you no longer wailing because you cannot swim in the river?" asked the witch-queen, speaking in the owl language.

"No, indeed," answered the gray owl. "For, as I watched a fish swimming in the water, a man caught it on a sharp hook, and the fish was killed. I believe I 'm safer in a tree."

"I believe so, too," said Zixi, and rode along more thoughtfully; for she remembered her own desire, and wondered if it would also prove foolish.

Just as they left the river-bank she noticed the old alligator sunning himself happily upon the bank.

"Of course," answered the alligator, opening one eye to observe his questioner.

"Have you ceased weeping because you cannot climb a tree?" asked the witch-queen.

"Of course," answered the alligator, opening one eye to observe his questioner. "For a boy climbed a tree near me yesterday and fell out of it and broke his leg. It is quite foolish to climb trees. I 'm sure I am safer in the water."

Zixi made no reply, but she agreed with the alligator, who called after her sleepily:

"Is n't it fortunate we cannot have everything we are stupid enough to wish for?"

Shortly afterward they left the river-bank and approached the lilac-grove, the witch-queen riding first through the trees to show the place where she had dropped the magic cloak. She knew it was near the little spring where she had gazed at her reflection in the water; but, although they searched over every inch of ground, they could discover no trace of the lost cloak.

"It is really too bad!" exclaimed Zixi, with vexation. "Some one must have come through the grove and taken the cloak away."

"But we must find it," said Bud, earnestly; "for otherwise I shall not be able to rescue my people from the Roly-Rogues."

"Let us inquire of every one we meet if they have seen the cloak," suggested Princess Fluff. "In that way we may discover who has taken it."

So they made a camp on the edge of the grove, and for two days they stopped and questioned all who passed that way. But none had ever seen or heard of a cloak like that described.

Finally an old shepherd came along, hobbling painfully after a flock of five sheep; for he suffered much from rheumatism.

"We have lost a beautiful cloak in the lilac-grove," said Zixi to the shepherd.

"When did you lose it?" asked the old man, pausing to lean upon his stick.

"Several days ago," returned the queen. "It was bright as the rainbow, and woven with threads finer than—"

"I know, I know!" interrupted the shepherd, "for I myself found it lying upon the ground beneath the lilac-trees."

"Hurrah!" cried Bud, gleefully; "at last we have found it!" And all the others were fully as delighted as he was.

"But where have you put the cloak?" inquired Zixi.

"Why, I gave it to Dame Dingle, who lives under the hill yonder," replied the man, pointing far away over the fields; "and she gave me in exchange some medicine for my rheumatism, which has made the pain considerably worse. So to-day I threw the bottle into the river."

They did not pause to listen further to the shepherd's talk, for all were now intent on reaching the cottage of Dame Dingle.

So the soldiers saddled the horses, and in a few minutes they were galloping away toward the hill. It was a long ride, over rough ground; but finally they came near the hill and saw a tiny, tumbledown cottage just at its foot.

Hastily dismounting, Bud, Fluff, and the queen rushed into the cottage, where a wrinkled old woman

"We have lost a beautiful cloak in the lilac grove,"
said Queen Zixi to the shepherd.

was bent nearly double over a crazy-quilt upon which she was sewing patches.

"Where is the cloak?" cried the three, in a breath.

The woman did not raise her head, but counted her stitches in a slow, monotonous tone.

"Sixteen — seventeen — eighteen —"

"Where is the magic cloak?" demanded Zixi, stamping her foot impatiently.

"Nineteen —" said Dame Dingle, slowly. "There! I 've broken my needle!"

"Answer us at once!" commanded Bud, sternly. "Where is the magic cloak?"

The woman paid no attention to him whatever. She carefully selected a new needle, threaded it after several attempts, and began anew to stitch the patch.

"Twenty!" she mumbled in a low voice; "twenty-one —"

But now Zixi snatched the work from her hands and exclaimed;

"If you do not answer at once I will give you a good beating!"

"That is all right," said the dame, looking up at them through her spectacles; "the patches take twenty-one stitches on each side, and if I lose my count I get mixed up. But it 's all right now. What do you want?"

"The cloak the old shepherd gave you," replied the queen, sharply.

"The pretty cloak with the bright colors?" asked

the dame, calmly.

"Yes! Yes!" answered the three, excitedly.

"Why, that very patch I was sewing was cut from that cloak," said Dame Dingle. "Is n't it lovely?

"Where is the cloak?" cried the three, in a breath.

And it brightens the rest of the crazy-quilt beautifully."

"Do you mean that you have cut up my magic cloak?" asked Fluff, in amazement, while the others were too horrified to speak.

"Certainly," said the woman. "The cloak was too fine for me to wear, and I needed something bright in my crazy-quilt. So I cut up half of the cloak and made patches of it."

The witch-queen gave a gasp, and sat down suddenly upon a rickety bench. Princess Fluff walked to the door and stood looking out, that the others might not see the tears of disappointment in her eyes. Bud alone stood scowling in front of the old dame, and presently he said to her, in a harsh tone:

"You ought to be smothered with your own crazy-quilt for daring to cut up the fairy cloak!"

"The fairy cloak!" echoed Dame Dingle. "What do you mean?"

"That cloak was a gift to my sister from the fairies," said Bud; "and it had a magic charm. Are n't you afraid the fairies will punish you for what you have done?"

Dame Dingle was greatly disturbed.

"How could I know it?" she asked, anxiously; "how could I know it was a magic cloak that old Edi gave to me?"

"Well, it was; and woven by the fairies themselves," retorted the boy. "And a whole nation is in danger because you have wickedly cut it up."

Dame Dingle tried to cry, to show that she was sorry and so escape punishment. She put her apron over her face, and rocked herself back and forth, and made an attempt to squeeze a tear out of her eyes.

Suddenly Zixi jumped up.

"Why, it is n't so bad, after all!" she exclaimed. "We can sew the cloak together again."

"Of course!" said Fluff, coming from the doorway. "Why did n't we think of that at once?"

"Where is the rest of the cloak?" demanded Zixi.

Dame Dingle went to a chest and drew forth the half of the cloak that had not been cut up. There was no doubt about its being the magic cloak. The golden thread Queen Lulea had woven could be seen plainly in the web, and the brilliant colors were as fresh and lovely as ever. But the flowing skirt of the cloak had been ruthlessly hacked by Dame Dingle's shears, and presented a sorry plight.

"Get us the patches you have cut!" commanded Zixi; and without a word the dame drew from her basket five small squares and then ripped from the crazy-quilt the one she had just sewn on.

"But this is n't enough," said Fluff, when she had spread the cloak upon the floor and matched the pieces. "Where is the rest of the cloak?"

"Why,—why—" stammered Dame Dingle, with hesitation, "I gave them away."

"Gave them away! Who got them?" said Bud.

"Why,—some friends of mine were here from the village last evening, and we traded patches, so each of us would have a variety for our crazy-quilts."

"Well?"

"And I gave each of them one of the patches from

the pretty cloak."

"Well, you *are* a ninny!" declared Bud, scornfully.

"Yes, your Majesty; I believe I am," answered Dame Dingle, meekly.

"We must go to the village and gather up those pieces," said Zixi. "Can you tell us the names of your friends?" she asked the woman.

"Of course," responded Dame Dingle; "they were Nancy Nink, Betsy Barx, Sally Sog, Molly Mitt, and Lucy Lum."

"Before we go to the village let us make Dame Dingle sew these portions of the cloak together," suggested Fluff.

The dame was glad enough to do this, and she threaded her needle at once. So deft and fine was her needlework that she mended the cloak most beautifully, so that from a short distance away no one could discover that the cloak had been darned. But a great square was still missing from the front, and our friends were now eager to hasten to the village.

"This will cause us some delay," said the witch-queen, more cheerfully; "but the cloak will soon be complete again, and then we can have our wishes."

Fluff took the precious cloak over her arm, and then they all mounted their horses and rode away toward the village, which Dame Dingle pointed out from her doorway. Zixi was sorry for the old creature, who had been more foolish than wicked; and the witch-queen left a bright gold piece in the woman's hand when she bade her good-by, which was worth more to Dame Dingle than three pretty cloaks.

The ground was boggy and uneven, so they were forced to ride slowly to the little village; but they arrived there at last, and began hunting for the old women who had received pieces of the magic cloak. They were easily found, and all seemed willing enough to give up their patches when the importance of the matter was explained to them.

At the witch-queen's suggestion, each woman fitted her patch to the cloak and sewed it on very neatly; but Lucy Lum, the last of the five, said to them:

"This is only half of the patch Dame Dingle gave me. The other part I gave to the miller's wife down in the valley where the river bends. But I am sure she will be glad to let you have it. See—it only requires that small piece to complete the cloak and make it as good as new."

It was true—the magic cloak, except for a small square at the bottom, was now complete; and such skilful needlewomen were these crazy-quilt makers that it was difficult to tell where it had been cut and afterward mended.

But the miller's wife must now be seen; so they all mounted the horses again, except Aunt Rivette, who grumbled that so much riding made her bones rattle and that she preferred to fly. Which she did, frightening the horses to such an extent with her wings that Bud made her keep well in advance of them.

They were all in good spirits now, for soon the magic cloak, almost as good as new, would be again in their possession; and Fluff and Bud had been greatly worried over the fate of their friends who had been left to the mercy of the terrible Roly-Rogues.

The path ran in a zigzag direction down into the valley; but at length it led the party to the mill, where old Rivette was found sitting in the doorway awaiting them.

The miller's wife, when summoned, came to them drying her hands on her apron, for she had been washing the dishes.

"We want to get the bright-colored patch Lucy Lum gave you," explained Fluff; "for it was part of my magic cloak, which the fairies gave to me, and this is the place where it must be sewn to complete the garment." And she showed the woman the cloak, with the square missing.

"I see," said the miller's wife, nodding her head; "and I am very sorry I cannot give you the piece to complete your cloak. But the fact is, I considered it too pretty for my crazy-quilt, so I gave it to my son for a necktie."

"And where is your son?" demanded Zixi.

"Oh, he is gone to sea, for he is a sailor. By this time he is far away upon the ocean."

Bud, Fluff, and the witch-queen looked at one another in despair.   This seemed, indeed, to destroy all their hopes; for the one portion of the cloak that they needed was far beyond their reach.

Nothing remained but for them to return to Zixi's palace and await the time when the miller's son should

"And where is your son?" demanded Zixi.

return from his voyage.   But before they went the queen said to the woman:

"When he returns you may tell your son that if he will bring to me the necktie you gave him, I will give him in return fifty gold pieces."

"And I will give him fifty more," said Bud, promptly.

"And I will give him enough ribbon to make fifty neckties," added Fluff.

The miller's wife was delighted at the prospect.

"Thank you! Thank you!" she exclaimed. "My boy's fortune is made. He can now marry Imogene Gubb and settle down on a farm, and give up the sea forever! And his neckties will be the envy of all the men in the country. As soon as he returns I will send him to you with the bit of the cloak which you need."

But Zixi was so anxious that nothing might happen to prevent the miller's son from returning the necktie, that she left two of her soldiers at the mill, with instructions to bring the man to her palace the instant he returned home.

As they rode away they were all very despondent over the ill luck of their journey.

"He may be drowned at sea," said Bud.

"Or he may lose the necktie on the voyage," said Fluff.

"Oh, a thousand things *might* happen," returned the queen; "but we need not make ourselves unhappy imagining them. Let us hope the miller's son will soon return and restore to us the missing patch." Which showed that Zixi had not lived six hundred and eighty-three years without gaining some wisdom.

Chapter XXII.

RUFFLES CARRIES THE SILVER VIAL.

When they were back at the witch-queen's palace in the city of Ix, the queen insisted that Bud and Fluff, with their Aunt Rivette, should remain her guests until the cloak could be restored to its former complete state. And, for fear something else might happen to the precious garment, a silver chest was placed in Princess Fluff's room and the magic cloak safely locked therein, the key being carried upon the chain around the girl's neck.

But their plans to wait patiently were soon interfered with by the arrival at Zixi's court of the talking dog, Ruffles, which had with much difficulty escaped from the Roly-Rogues.

Ruffles brought to them so sad and harrowing a tale of the sufferings of the five high counselors and all the people of Noland at the hands of the fierce Roly-Rogues, that Princess Fluff wept bitterly for her friends, and Bud became so cross and disagreeable that even Zixi was provoked with him.

"Something really must be done," declared the queen. "I'll brew a magical mess in my witch-kettle to-night, and see if I can find a way to destroy those detestable Roly-Rogues."

Indeed, she feared the creatures would some day find their way into Ix; so when all the rest of those in the palace were sound asleep, Zixi worked her magic spell, and from the imps she summoned she obtained advice how to act in order to get rid of the Roly-Rogues.

Next morning she questioned Ruffles carefully.

"What do the Roly-Rogues eat?" she asked.

"Everything," said the dog; "for they have no judgment, and consume buttons and hairpins as eagerly as they do food. But there is one thing they are really fond of, and that is soup. They oblige old Tollydob, the lord high general, who works in the palace kitchen, to make them a kettle of soup every morning; and this they all eat as if they were half starving."

"Very good!" exclaimed the witch-queen, with pleasure. "I think I see a way of ridding all No-land of these monsters. Here is a Silver Vial filled with a magic liquid. I will tie it around your neck, and you must return to the city of Nole and carry the vial to Tollydob, the lord high general. Tell him that on Thursday morning, when he makes the kettle of soup, he must put the contents of the vial into the compound. But let no one taste it afterward except the Roly-Rogues."

"And what then?" asked Ruffles, curiously.

"Then I will myself take charge of the monsters;

and I have reason to believe the good citizens of Noland will no longer find themselves slaves."

"All right," said the dog. "I will do as you bid
me; for I long to free my master and have revenge
on the Roly-Rogues."

Queen Zixi tied the silver vial to the dog's neck.

So Queen Zixi tied the Silver Vial to the dog's
neck by means of a broad ribbon, and he started at
once to return to Nole.

And when he had gone, the queen summoned all
her generals and bade them assemble the entire army
and prepare to march into Noland again. Only this

time, instead of being at enmity with the people of Noland, the army of Ix was to march to their relief; and instead of bearing swords and spears, each man bore a coil of strong rope.

He started at once to return to Nole.

"For," said Zixi, "swords and spears are useless where the Roly-Rogues are concerned, as nothing can pierce their tough, rubber-like bodies. And more nations have been conquered by cunning than by force of arms."

Bud and Fluff, not knowing what the witch-queen meant to do, were much disturbed by these preparations to march upon the Roly-Rogues. The monsters had terrified them so greatly that they dreaded to meet with them again, and Bud declared that the safest plan was to remain in Zixi's kingdom and await thc coming of the miller's son with the necktie.

"But," remonstrated Zixi, "in the meantime your people are suffering terribly."

"I know," said Bud; "and it nearly drives me frantic to think of it. But they will be no better off if we try to fight the Roly-Rogues and are ourselves made slaves."

"Why not try the magic cloak as it is," suggested the little princess, "and see if it won't grant wishes as before? There's only a small piece missing, and it may not make any difference with the power the fairies gave to it."

"Hooray!" shouted Bud. "That's a good idea. It's a magic cloak just the same, even if there is a chunk cut out of it."

Zixi agreed that it was worth a trial, so the cloak was taken from the silver casket and brought into the queen's reception-room.

"Let us try it on one of your maids of honor, first," said Fluff; "and, if it grants her wish, we will know the cloak has lost none of its magic powers. Then you and Bud may both make your wishes."

"Very well," returned the queen, and she summoned one of her maids.

"I am going to lend you my cloak," said the princess to the maid; "and while you wear it you must make a wish."

She threw the cloak over the girl's shoulders, and after a moment's thought the maid said:

"I wish for a bushel of candies."

"Fudge!" said Bud, scornfully.

"No; all kinds of candies," answered the maid of honor.   But, although they watched her intently, the

"And may I wish for anything I desire?" she asked eagerly.

wish failed absolutely, for no bushel of candies appeared in sight.

"Let us try it again," suggested Fluff, while the others wore disappointed expressions.   "It was a foolish wish, anyhow; and perhaps the fairies did not care to grant it."

So another maid was called and given the cloak to wear.

"And may I wish for anything I desire?" she asked eagerly.

"Of course," answered the princess; "but, as you can have but one wish, you must choose something sensible."

"Oh, I will!" declared the maid. "I wish I had yellow hair and blue eyes."

"Why did you wish that?" asked Fluff, angrily, for the girl had pretty brown hair and eyes.

"Because the young man I am going to marry says he likes blondes better than brunettes," answered the maid, blushing.

But her hair did not change its color, for all the wish; and the maid said, with evident disappointment:

"Your magic cloak seems to be a fraud."

"It does not grant foolish wishes," returned the princess, as she dismissed her.

When the maid had gone Zixi asked:

"Well, are you satisfied?"

"Yes," acknowledged Fluff. "The cloak will not grant wishes unless it is complete. We must wait for the sailorman's necktie."

"Then my army shall march to-morrow morning," said the queen, and she went away to give the order to her generals.

Chapter XXIII.

THE DESTRUCTION OF THE MONSTERS.

It was Tuesday when the army of Ix started upon its second march into Noland. With it were the witch-queen, King Bud, Princess Fluff, and Aunt Rivette. At evening they encamped on the bank of the river, and on Wednesday the army was ferried across, and marched up the side of the mountain that separated them from the valley of Noland. By night they had reached the summit of the mountain; but they did not mount upon the ridge, for fear they might be seen by the Roly-Rogues.

Zixi commanded them all to remain quietly behind the ridge, and they lighted no fires and spoke only in whispers.

And, although so many thousands of men lay close to the valley of Noland, not a sound came from them to warn the monsters that an enemy was near.

Thursday morning dawned bright and pleasant, and as soon as the sun was up the Roly-Rogues came crowding around the palace kitchen, demanding that old Tollydob hurry the preparation of their soup.

This the general did, trembling in spite of his ten feet of stature; for if they were kept waiting the monsters were liable to prod his flesh with their thorns.

But Tollydob did not forget to empty the contents

And the dog Ruffles ran through the city, crying to every
Roly-Rogue he met: "Hurry and get your soup."

of the Silver Vial into the soup, as the dog Ruffles
had told him to do; and soon it was being ladled out
to the Roly-Rogues by Jikki, the four high counselors, and a dozen other enslaved officers of King Bud.

And the dog Ruffles ran through the city, crying to
every Roly-Rogue he met: "Hurry and get your soup
before it is gone.   It is especially good this morning!"

So every Roly-Rogue in the valley hurried to the palace kitchen for soup; and there were so many that it was noon before the last were served, while these became so impatient that they abused their slaves in a sad manner.

Yet, even while the last were eating, those who had earlier partaken of the soup lay around the palace sound asleep and snoring loudly; for the contents of the Silver Vial had the effect of sending all of them to sleep within an hour, and rendering them wholly unconscious for a period of ten hours.

All through the city the Roly-Rogues lay asleep; and, as they always withdrew their heads and limbs into their bodies when they slumbered, they presented a spectacle of thousands of huge balls lying motionless.

When the big kettle was finally empty and the lord high general paused to wipe the perspiration from his brow, the last of the Roly-Rogues were rolling over on their backs from the effects of the potion which the witch-queen brewed and placed in the Silver Vial.

Aunt Rivette had been flying over the city since early morning; and although the Roly-Rogues had been too intent upon their breakfast to notice her, the old woman's sharp eyes had watched everything that took place below.

Now, when all the monsters had succumbed to the witch-potion, Aunt Rivette flew back to the mountain where the army of Ix was hidden, and carried the news to the witch-queen.

Zixi at once ordered her generals to advance, and the entire army quickly mounted the summit of the ridge and ran down the side of the mountain to the gates of the city.

All through the city the Roly-Rogues lay asleep.

The people, who saw that something unusual was taking place, greeted Bud and Fluff and the witch-queen with shouts of gladness; and even Aunt Rivette, when she flew down among them, was given three hearty cheers.

But there was no time for joyous demonstrations while the streets and public squares were cluttered with the sleeping bodies of the terrible Roly-Rogues. The army of Ix lost no time in carrying out their queen's instructions; and as soon as they entered the city they took the long ropes they carried and wound them fast about the round bodies of the monsters, securely fastening their heads and limbs into their forms so that they could not stick them out again.

Their enemies being thus rendered helpless, the people renewed their shouts of joy and gratitude, and eagerly assisted the soldiers of Ix in rolling all the Roly-Rogues outside the gates and to a wide ledge of the mountain.

The lord high general and all the other counselors threw away their aprons and tools of servitude and dressed themselves in their official robes. The soldiers of Tollydob's army ran for their swords and pikes, and the women unlocked their doors and trooped into the streets of Nole for the first time since the descent of the monsters.

But the task of liberation was not yet accomplished. All the Roly-Rogues had to be rolled up the side of the mountain to the topmost ridge, and so great was the bulk of their bodies that it took five or six men to roll each one to the mountain-top; and even then they were obliged to stop frequently to rest.

All the Roly-Rogues were thus rolled into the river,
where they bobbed up and down in the water.

But as soon as they got a Roly-Rogue to the ridge they gave it a push and sent it bounding down the other side of the mountain until it fell into the big river flowing swiftly below.

During the afternoon all the Roly-Rogues were thus dumped into the river, where they bobbed up and down in the water, spinning around and bumping against one another until the current carried them out of sight on their journey to the sea. It was rumored later that they had reached an uninhabited island where they harm no one except themselves.

" I 'm glad they floated," said Zixi, as she stood upon the mountain ridge and watched the last of the monsters float out of sight; "for if they had sunk they would have filled up the river, there were so many of them."

It was evening when Noland at last became free from her terrible tyrants; and the citizens illuminated the entire city that they might spend the night in feasting and rejoicing over their freedom. The soldiers of Ix were embraced and made much of; and at all the feasts they were the honored guests, while the people of Noland pledged them their sincere friendship forever.

King Bud took possession of the royal palace again, and Jikki bustled about and prepared a grand banquet for the king's guests, — although the old valet grumbled a great deal because his six solemn servants would not assist in waiting upon any one but himself.

The Roly-Rogues had destroyed many things, but the servants of the palace managed to quickly clear away the rubbish and to decorate the banquet-hall handsomely.

Bud placed the beautiful witch-queen upon his right hand and showed her great honor, for he was really very grateful for her assistance in rescuing his country from the invaders.

The feasting and dancing lasted far into the night; but when at last the people sought their beds they knew they might rest peacefully and free from care, for the Roly-Rogues had gone forever.

Chapter XXIV.

THE SAILORMAN'S RETURN.

Next day the witch-queen returned with her army to the city of Ix, to await the coming of the sailorman with the necktie, and King Bud set about getting his kingdom into running order again.

The lord high purse-bearer dug up his magic purse, and Bud ordered him to pay the shopkeepers full value for everything the Roly-Rogues had destroyed. The merchants were thus enabled to make purchases of new stocks of goods; and although all travelers had for many days kept away from Noland, for fear of the monsters, caravans now flocked in vast numbers to the city of Nole with rich stores of merchandise to sell, so that soon the entire city looked like a huge bazaar.

Bud also ordered a gold piece given to the head of every family; and this did no damage to the ever-filled royal purse, while it meant riches to the poor people who had suffered so much.

Princess Fluff had carried her silver chest back to the palace of her brother, and in it lay, carefully folded, the magic cloak. Being now fearful of losing it, she warned Jikki to allow no one to enter the room in which lay the silver chest, except with her full consent, explaining to him the value of the cloak.

"And was it this cloak I wore when I wished for half a dozen servants?" asked the old valet.

"Yes," answered Fluff; "Aunt Rivette bade you return it to me, and you were so careless of it that nearly all the high counselors used it before I found it again."

"Then," said Jikki, heedless of the reproof, "will your Highness please use the cloak to rid me of these stupid servants? They are continually at my heels, waiting to serve me; and I am so busy myself serving others that those six young men almost drive me distracted. It would n't be so bad if they would serve any one else; but they claim they are my servants alone, and refuse to wait upon even his Majesty the king."

"Sometime I will try to help you," answered Fluff; "but I shall not use the cloak again until the miller's son returns from his voyage at sea."

So Jikki was forced to wait as impatiently as the others for the sailorman, and his servants had now become such a burden upon him that he grumbled every time he looked around and saw them standing in a stiff line behind him.

Aunt Rivette again took possession of her rooms at the top of the palace; and although Bud, grateful for her courage in saving him and his sister from the Roly-Rogues, would gladly have given her handsomer apartments, the old woman preferred to be near the roof, where she could take flight into the air whenever it pleased her to go out.

With her big wings and her power to fly as a bird, she was the envy of all the old gossips she had known in the days when she worked as a laundress; and now she would often alight upon the door-step of some humble friend and tell of the wonderful adventures she had encountered.

This never failed to surround her with an admiring circle of listeners, and Aunt Rivette derived far more pleasure from her tattle than from living in a palace with her nephew the king.

The kingdom of Noland soon took on a semblance of its former prosperity, and the Roly-Rogues were only remembered with shudders of repugnance, and spoken of in awed whispers.

And so the days wore away until late in the autumn, when, one morning, a mounted soldier from Queen Zixi dashed into Nole and rode furiously up to the palace gate.

"The sailorman is found!" he shouted, throwing himself from his horse and bowing low before little King Bud, who had come out to meet him.

"Good," remarked Bud.

"The Queen of Ix is even now riding to your Majesty's city with a large escort surrounding the sailorman," continued the soldier.

"And has he the necktie?" asked Bud, eagerly.

"He is wearing it, your Majesty," answered the

man; "but he refuses to give it to any one but the Princess Fluff."

"That's all right," said the king; and, reëntering the palace, he ordered Jikki to make prep-

F. RICHARDSON

"The sailorman is found!" he shouted.

arations to receive the witch-queen and her retinue.

When Zixi came to the city gates she found General Tollydob, in a gorgeous new uniform, waiting to escort her to the palace. The houses were gay with flags and streamers; bands were playing; and on each side of the street along which the witch-queen rode were lines of soldiers to keep the way clear of the crowding populace.

Behind the queen came the sailorman, carefully guarded by Zixi's most trusted soldiers. He looked uneasy at so great a reception, and rode his horse as awkwardly as a sailor might.

So the cavalcade came to the palace, which was thronged with courtiers and ladies in waiting.

Zixi and the sailorman were ushered into the great throne-room, where King Bud, wearing his ermine robe and jeweled crown, sat gravely upon his throne, with Princess Fluff beside him.

"Your Majesty," began the witch-queen, bowing prettily, "I have brought you the sailorman at last. He has just returned from his voyage, and my soldiers captured him at his mother's cottage by the mill. But he refuses to give the necktie to any one except the Princess Fluff."

"I am the Princess Fluff," said Meg to the sailor; "and your necktie is part of my magic cloak. So please give it back to me."

The sailor shifted uneasily from one foot to the other.

"My mother told me," he finally said, "that King Bud would give me fifty gold pieces for it, and the Queen of Ix would give me another fifty gold pieces, and that your Highness would give me fifty neckties."

"That is all true," returned Fluff; "so here are the fifty neckties."

Tillydib, the lord high purse-bearer, counted out fifty gold pieces, and Zixi's treasurer counted out another fifty, and all were given to the sailorman.

"This is not the necktie your mother gave you!"

Then the miller's son unfastened the necktie from about his collar and handed it to Fluff.

During the murmur of satisfaction that followed, the girl unlocked her silver chest, which Jikki had brought, and drew out the magic cloak. Lifting the skirt of the garment, she attempted to fit the sailor's

necktie into the place it should go; and then, while
every one looked on with breathless interest, the girl
lifted a white face to the sailorman and exclaimed:

"This is not the necktie your mother gave you!"

For a moment there was silence, while the assemblage glared angrily upon the sailor. Then the king,
rising from his seat, demanded:

"Are you sure, Fluff? Are you sure of that?"

"Of course I'm sure," said the girl; "it is neither
the shape nor the color of the missing patch."

Bud turned to the now trembling sailor.

"Why have you tried to deceive us?" he asked
sternly.

"Oh, your Majesty!" returned the man, wringing
his hands miserably, "I lost the necktie in a gale at
sea, for I knew nothing of its value. And when I
came home my mother told me of all the gold you
had offered for its return, and advised me to deceive
you by wearing another necktie. She said you would
never know the difference."

"Your mother is a foolish woman, as well as dis-
honest," answered Bud; "and you shall both be severely punished. Tellydeb," he continued, addressing
the lord high executioner, "take this man to prison,
and see that he is fed on bread and water until further orders."

"Not so!" exclaimed a sweet voice near the king;
and then all looked up to see the beautiful Lulea,
queen of the fairies, standing beside the throne.

Chapter XXV.

THE FAIRY QUEEN.

Every eye was now fixed upon the exquisite form of the fairy queen, which shed a glorious radiance throughout the room, and filled every heart with an awe and admiration not unmingled with fear.

"The magic cloak was woven by my band," said the fairy, speaking so distinctly that all could hear the words; "and our object was to bring relief to suffering mortals—not to add to their worries. Some good the cloak has accomplished, I am sure; but also has it been used foolishly, and to no serious purpose. Therefore I, who gave the cloak, shall now take it away. The good that has been done shall remain; but the foolish wishes granted shall now be canceled." With these words, she turned and lightly lifted the shimmering magic garment from the lap of the princess.

"One moment, please!" cried Bud, eagerly. "Cannot I have my wish? I waited until I could wish wisely, you know; and then the cloak would n't work."

With a smile, Lulea threw the cloak over the boy's shoulders.

"Wish!" said she.

"I wish," announced Bud, gravely, "that I may become the best king that Noland has ever had!"

"Your wish is granted," returned the fairy, sweetly; "and it shall be the last wish fulfilled through the magic cloak."

But now Zixi rushed forward and threw herself upon her knees before the fairy.

"Oh, your Majesty—" she began eagerly; but Lulea instantly silenced her with an abrupt gesture.

"Plead not to me, Queen of Ix!" said the dainty immortal, drawing back from Zixi's prostrate form. "You know that we fairies do not approve of witchcraft. However long your arts may permit you to live, you must always beware a mirror!"

Zixi gave a sob and buried her pretty face in her hands; and it was Fluff whose tender heart prompted her to raise the witch-queen and try to comfort her.

For a moment all present had looked at Zixi. When their eyes again sought the form of the fairy, Lulea had vanished, and with her disappeared forever from Noland the magic cloak.

Some important changes had been wrought through the visit of the fairy. Jikki's six servants were gone, to the old valet's great delight. The ten-foot general had shrunken to six feet in height, Lulea having generously refrained from reducing old Tollydob to his former short stature. Ruffles, to the grief of the lord high steward, could no longer talk; but Tallydab comforted himself with the knowledge that his dog

"I wish," gravely announced Bud, "that I may become
the best king that Noland has ever had!"

"Oh, your Majesty—!" she began eagerly.

could at least understand every word addressed to him. The lord high executioner found he could no longer reach farther than other men; but the royal purse of old Tillydib remained ever filled, which assured the future prosperity of the kingdom of Noland.

As for Zixi, she soon became reconciled to her fate, and returned to Ix to govern her country with her former liberality and justice.

The last wish granted by the magic cloak was doubtless the most beneficial and far-reaching of all; for King Bud ruled many years with exceeding wisdom and gentleness, and was greatly beloved by each and every one of his admiring subjects.

The cheerfulness and sweet disposition of Princess Fluff became renowned throughout the world, and when she grew to womanhood many brave and handsome princes from other countries came to Nole to sue for her heart and hand. One of these she married, and reigned as queen of a great nation in after years, winning quite as much love and respect from her people as his loyal subjects bestowed upon her famous brother, King Bud of Noland.

THE  END